ALIEN GAME

CASTALIA HOUSE

SCIENCE FICTION
Superluminary by John C. Wright
City Beyond Time by John C. Wright
Back From the Dead by Rolf Nelson
Mutiny in Space by Rod Walker
Alien Game by Rod Walker
Young Man's War by Rod Walker

MILITARY SCIENCE FICTION
There Will Be War Volumes I and II ed. Jerry Pournelle
Starship Liberator by David VanDyke and B. V. Larson
Battleship Indomitable by David VanDyke and B. V. Larson
The Eden Plague by David VanDyke
Reaper's Run by David VanDyke
Skull's Shadows by David VanDyke

FANTASY
Summa Elvetica by Vox Day
A Throne of Bones by Vox Day
A Sea of Skulls by Vox Day
The Green Knight's Squire by John C. Wright
Iron Chamber of Memory by John C. Wright
Awake in the Night by John C. Wright

FICTION
An Equation of Almost Infinite Complexity by J. Mulrooney
The Missionaries by Owen Stanley
The Promethean by Owen Stanley
Brings the Lightning by Peter Grant
Rocky Mountain Retribution by Peter Grant
Hitler in Hell by Martin van Creveld

NON-FICTION
SJWs Always Lie by Vox Day
SJWs Always Double Down by Vox Day
The LawDog Files by LawDog
The LawDog Files: African Adventures by LawDog
Equality: The Impossible Quest by Martin van Creveld
A History of Strategy by Martin van Creveld

ALIEN GAME

ROD WALKER

CASTALIA HOUSE

Alien Game

Rod Walker

Published by Castalia House
Tampere, Finland
www.castaliahouse.com

Cover: Lars Braad Andersen
Editor: Vox Day

ISBN: 978-952-7065-62-4

Contents

Chapter 1

It's Good To Have Friends

There are two things you have to understand.

First, I never, ever should have listened to my girlfriend.

Second, my Uncle Morgan hated the Ecology Ministry. He wasn't a violent man, but if EcoMin was on fire, Uncle Morgan wouldn't have crossed the street to relieve himself on it. He would have driven home, picked up a lawn chair and a cooler of beers, driven back and enjoyed the show.

Actually, on that topic, there's a third thing I should probably mention.

I live on the planet of New Princeton, and New Princeton is the kind of world where the right bribe to the right person will get you out of anything. The government is a dictatorship, and while I wouldn't say it's a benevolent dictatorship, it's probably not what you're thinking of either. It's more of an incompetent and passive-aggressive one.

There are worse places.

There are planets where if you don't pray to the right god seven times a day, they stone you to death in the public square, and other planets where if you don't get up at dawn to applaud the Supreme Leader's morning rant against reactionary wreckers, they starve you to death in a labor camp.

New Princeton isn't that kind of place. The unwritten rule is that so long as you pay your taxes, bribe the right officials when necessary, and don't get involved in politics, the Acadarchy will let you be. And even if you get involved in politics, they don't send the police to beat you to death or put you up against a wall and shoot you. No, what happens is that you suddenly find yourself on the business end of a bunch of lawsuits, the inspectors from CareMin and EcoMin start leveling fines for various infractions, RevMin discovers you've been underpaying your taxes, and eventually you go bankrupt, find yourself on Basic Income, and aren't allowed to vote any more. That's that. Mr. Royale says that it's all very civilized, and compared to places that have Supreme Leaders I suppose it is, but Mr. Royale says a lot of things like that.

Anyhow, about that girlfriend.

Her name was Theresa, and the way she looked pretty much shut down my brain. I wanted to impress her so I did a lot of stupid things. In hindsight, I probably should have thought more about what it meant that she was so easily impressed by such stupid stuff.

Mr. Royale warned me that she was trouble, but I only met her because of him, so you could almost say it was all his fault.

Yes. It was definitely his fault. All this began the day I met Mr. Royale.

It was a Tuesday in late spring, right after the first planting was done. Uncle Morgan owns thirty thousand acres of prime farmland, with the title to the land dating all the way back to when our first ancestor signed New Princeton's colonial charter fifteen centuries ago. He was always worried EcoMin would find a way to screw him out of the land, but they hadn't managed it yet, and thanks to the miracle of modern robotics, thirty thousand acres was just profitable enough that he could operate the farm without outside investors. Ever since my parents had died, I had more or less worked for Uncle Morgan, and I was driving my electric truck along the outer edges of the farm, stopping every so often to do a maintenance check on the irrigation pumps. Uncle Morgan hated mechanical things, but I didn't, so he often dumped the maintenance on me.

I saw Mr. Royale on my fifth stop, and I was so surprised that I just stared at him.

I never saw people on the farm. New Princeton is the kind of place where 98 percent of the population lives packed into twenty-five different megapolitan areas scattered around the globe, and everyone who lives outside the cities is either a farmer, an EcoMin employee, or a worker on the rail links between the cities. So when I saw a man in a white suit running for his life down the dirt road, I was too astonished to say anything.

Then I saw why he was running for his life.

Three fangwolves were after him.

I vaguely remembered from my biology study module that fangwolves were native to New Princeton, that they had been the apex predator long before humans had ever shown up. Despite the massive changes we had brought to the planet's ecology, the fangwolves continued to thrive, probably because they could eat almost anything that had protein in its makeup. They had almost been wiped out during the colonization, but as more of the planet's population had moved into the cities, the fangwolves had made a comeback.

Now the vicious things were everywhere, which was why I never went out without a rifle.

I sprinted for the bed of the truck and snatched my rifle out of its rack. It was a Mordecai Sportsman .30 hunting rifle that could hold nine rounds, and while that caliber of bullet wasn't useful against some of the bigger predators that wandered the wilderness of New Princeton, it would work just fine for fangwolves. I flipped the safety off, raised the gun to my shoulder, and took aim, my finger settling on the trigger.

The fangwolves gained on the fleeing man, and I took a deep, calming breath and started shooting.

My first shot was a good one. It thumped right into the side of the first fangwolf and hurled the beast over on its side. Despite their name, fangwolves didn't actually have any fur, though they did have six clawed legs and fangs like long, curved knives. All six of those legs thrashed madly about as the fangwolf died. My second shot smacked into the road with a puff of dust, and the remaining two fangwolves stopped, confused by the bizarre behavior of their fallen companion.

Their hesitation let me drill the second one right through the skull.

The third one suddenly whirled and came right at me, all six legs driving it forward with terrific speed. Animals descended from the species of ancient Earth still retained their ancestral fear of humans. Animals native to alien planets did not, and some of them, like the fangwolves, reacted to the sight and smell of humans with ferocious rage.

Fortunately, this was far from my first encounter with the creatures, so I just took careful aim, then shot the charging fangwolf in the chest. It tumbled head-over-tail to a halt about twenty yards away, its bluish blood seeping into the dirt.

I looked around, my rifle at the ready, but no more fangwolves seemed to be prowling around the dirt road.

"You okay?" I said, walking forward towards the man in the white suit.

He stared at me. He had been sprinting at a pretty good clip, but he wasn't breathing all that hard, and he didn't look as frightened as I would have expected, given that he had nearly been ripped apart by fangwolves. I guessed he was about thirty-five, and he was obviously from one of the cities since no one out here dressed in white suits. My next thought was that he worked for EcoMin or TransMin, but the nearest rail line was forty miles away, and the EcoMin agents usually traveled in caravans.

"Son, I know a thing or two about firearms," said the man. Definitely, a city guy—his accent pegged him as someone from Wilson City, the nearest megapolis to Uncle Morgan's farm. "That was excellent shooting."

I shrugged. "Getting bitten by one of those things isn't fun." I tugged on my left sleeve to reveal the nasty scar on my forearm. "So I'm real motivated not to repeat the experience."

"A sensible policy," said the man. "Were you aware that it's illegal to shoot fangwolves without a permit?"

I eyed him. Maybe he was from EcoMin. Was he looking for a bribe? "What about it?"

The man blinked, and then laughed. "Ah! I see! No, young man, you misunderstand me. You just saved my life, I am in your debt, and I always remember my debts. I just wondered if you might happen to have a convenient way of disposing of the carcasses. If not, I have the facilities to take care of it."

"I do," I said. "Well, my uncle does. He's got an organic decompiler at one of the barns. I'll dump the bodies in there, and it'll render them down into fertilizer." I eyed him. "That going to be a problem?"

"Certainly not," said the man. "If I help you load them into your vehicle, will you give me a lift? I'm afraid mine broke down about three miles that way, and I was looking for help."

I frowned. "Couldn't you call someone?"

He tapped his jacket. "No signal out here."

"Oh, yeah," I said. "It's spotty in these parts. Depends on the weather. Well, if you help me load those things into the truck, I'll give you a lift."

He grinned. "My suit's already ruined, so why not?" He extended his hand. "Name's Ian Royale."

I shifted my rifle to my other hand and shook his hand. "Sam Hammond, Mr. Royale." I set the rifle down, grabbed one end of the nearest dead fangwolf, and he took the other. "What brings you out here?"

"Business," he said, lifting the dead animal. Together we dumped its carcass into the back of the truck.

"What kind of business?" I said. He definitely wasn't with EcoMin or any of the other Acadarchy departments, I was sure of that. Otherwise, he would have commandeered my truck by now.

"This and that," said Mr. Royale. That made me wonder if he was a drug dealer. "Basically, my business is in favors."

"Favors?" I laughed as we grabbed the second dead animal. "You in with one of the cartels?"

"Not at all. You see, Mr. Hammond, there are two kinds of people in this world or any other world. People who have things they don't want, and people who want things they don't have. That applies to most aliens as well, though that is not the point. People owe me favors, and I use them to bring together the two kinds of people. And then I collect a small fee for my services, and everybody goes home happy."

"So how's that work?" I said.

He explained, rather more openly than I'd expected. Mr. Royale, as I soon learned, liked to talk, and he talked during the entire drive to the barn with the decompiler. He had started forty-seven different business ventures, and of them, forty-three had failed either completely or catastrophically. However, the four that succeeded had done very well. In fact…

"Wait," I said. "You're the guy who owns the KwikBreet machines?"

"Yes indeed," said Mr. Royale.

"My uncle loves KwikBreets," I said. "Every time we go to Wilson City he eats like three of the things. He really likes the teriyaki ones for some reason."

"I knew those would go over well," said Mr. Royale. "My investors, they thought I was nuts, but the teriyaki-flavored ones are the best sellers. God intended burritos to have teriyaki flavor, I tell you."

I frowned. "There must be like a thousand KwikBreet machines in Wilson City."

"One thousand four hundred ninety-six," said Mr. Royale. "I'm hoping to expand the franchise to Clinton City. Which is why I was on my way to Rusk Station, as it happens. The station master owes me a few favors, and I was hoping to trade in on them to reduce my shipping expenses."

"I see," I said.

That was the thing about Mr. Royale, other than that he liked to talk a lot. He wasn't exactly a mobster. None of his business ventures were illegal, and he scrupulously adhered to the letter of the law. He did, however, completely ignore its spirit, and carefully exploited every possible loophole to its maximum extent. In that, he reminded me a lot of Uncle

Morgan, who liked to say that the law was what EcoMin used to screw over the small farmer. If the Acadarchy didn't want him to ship his goods via rail to avoid the air tax, or hire his employees as contractors, or to incorporate some of his companies in Jackson City because Jackson City had the lowest fees, Mr. Royale said, then they ought to change the law. If they didn't, that was their problem.

"What are your other three businesses?" I said, intrigued now. We were almost to the barn. "The ones that worked, I mean."

"Ha!" said Mr. Royale. "Usually, people want to hear about the failures. One was a software company that developed a new middleware database."

"Huh?"

"Software that talks to other software," said Mr. Royale. "I sold that company, though I still have a stake in it. I also have a food distributorship, which comes in handy for KwikBreet. I have a cleaning robot rental business in Wilson City that does very well. Most people are too lazy to clean their own apartments…"

"So you find people and sell them what they want," I said.

"Exactly," said Mr. Royale. "The last business is a safari company."

"Safari?" I said.

"You know the one habitable planet in the Arborea system?" said Mr. Royale.

"Sort of," I said. I didn't pay much attention to the news.

"Well, the Acadarchy agreed to let a private company run hunting trips to it, and I got one of the contracts as a favor," said Mr. Royale. "The Ecology Ministry had a fit. If the Ecocrats got their way, all colonization efforts throughout the

Thousand Worlds would be shut down and then we'd collectively kill ourselves to preserve the pristine natural landscape on every planet… but I digress. The Acadarchy needs the money, so that's that. In a year or two, I'll be ferrying rich tourists to Arborea…"

"In exchange for a reasonable cut?" I said.

"Exactly," said Mr. Royale.

"All these companies," I said. "You must be rich."

Mr. Royale laughed. "You'd think so, but I've lost more money than I've made. On paper, it's a lot, but in practice, most of it is tied up in the companies. Which is why I often do things myself, such as dumping fangwolf carcasses into organic decompilers." He craned his neck. "Is that your uncle's barn?"

"One of them, anyway," I said, steering the truck into the gravel lot next to the barn and shutting down the engine. "He keeps some of his autonomous tractors here. Deserted right now, but you should visit around harvest time. Uncle Morgan hires on temporary workers then, and all the tractors are going 24/7. Heck of a time keeping them all operational."

"That's what you do here?" said Mr. Royale. "Tractor repair?"

I shrugged. "This and that. Mechanical stuff, mostly. I like fixing things. It's Uncle Morgan's farm, but my dad worked for him doing the same kind of stuff before the accident." Hopefully, that would defuse the awkward questions about what had happened to my parents. I hated talking about it, and I hated the same stupid question and the same boring platitudes every single time.

Mr. Royale was clever enough to pick up on that. "I see. And you enjoy this sort of work?"

I shrugged again. "It's what I'm good at. Someone needs to know how to fix a drive motivator, change a tire, or reboot a drone OS."

"Indeed," said Mr. Royale. "You seem a talented young man, Mr. Hammond."

We got out of the truck and started dumping the fangwolf carcasses into the organic decompiler. The smell was horrible, of course, but it also meant a few extra kilograms of free fertilizer, so I didn't complain. The endlessly rising cost of fertilizer was one of Uncle Morgan's favorite topics.

"I'll give you a lift to Rusk Station," I said once we finished.

"There's no need to put yourself out," said Mr. Royale. "We seem to have signal here, and I can summon a ride."

"Nah," I said. "Rusk Station's only four miles out of my way, and I've got to check on the irrigation controller on the north field. I'll drop you off."

"That's very kind," said Mr. Royale.

I grinned. "Though if you wanted to give me a voucher for some free KwikBreets the next time I'm in Wilson City, I would not complain."

Mr. Royale laughed. "You have it." He reached into his coat and produced a hundred-credit gift card good in any Kwik-Breet machine in the Wilson City area.

"Hey, thanks," I said. "My uncle will love that."

"Also, this," said Mr. Royale, handing me another card. This one was made of cardboard and held a comms number and a digital address.

"What's this?" I said.

"If you ever find yourself in need of employment," said Mr. Royale, "give me a call."

I blinked. "You're offering me a job?"

"You're a clever young fellow, Hammond," said Mr. Royale. "And exceptionally cool under pressure, as those dead fang-wolves will attest." He waved a hand in front of his nose. The organic decompiler is efficient and a great way to make fertilizer, but it smells like the locker room of hell. "There is always use for cool-headed individuals in business."

"I'll have to think it over," I said. "And talk to my uncle."

"Do that," said Mr. Royale. "But if you decide you're interested," he tapped the card, "you know how to get in touch with me."

Later that evening I told Uncle Morgan what had happened.

He listened without interrupting. My uncle was a big man, both strong from work and fat from eating too much, with graying hair and beard and arms that looked like logs. He usually wore dust-stained work clothes, a can of beer in his right fist. I could remember times when I had seen him without alcohol close at hand, but maybe only a dozen times, and none since my parents had died. His nose was red from constant drinking, his eyes were bloodshot. As far as I knew, his liver hadn't gone yet, which was just as well. If he needed a new liver, he would have to go to a Care Ministry transplant center, and he would rather die than do that.

"What do you think?" I said.

Uncle Morgan. "You should take the job." He grunted and took a long drink from the can, then shook his head. "Not that I want to lose you. You've been useful to have around. If I had my way, I'd give the farm to you." His mouth twisted with the old bitterness. "But the ecocrats won't let me."

I said nothing. Uncle Morgan held title to the farm, our family's legal claim to the land dating back to when the first settlers had colonized New Princeton. But the law dictated that the farm could only pass to Uncle Morgan's children. My father had been Uncle Morgan's younger brother and if Uncle Morgan had died first, my father would have inherited the farm, and then I would have inherited it in turn. But my parents died in a train derailment and Uncle Morgan had no children. That meant that when he died, EcoMin would claim that the land had reverted to the Acadarchy. They had been doing this sort of thing for centuries, gradually eating away at the independent farmers one by one and selling their lands to the giant agribusiness conglomerates, on the ridiculous grounds that doing so resulted in more ecologically friendly farming.

Uncle Morgan sighed. "There's no future for you here. You're eighteen now, and can make your own decisions. You should start building yourself a life so you have something to fall back on when we lose the farm. Better go to the city and make your fortune there. Find a way off New Princeton if you can and head for someplace less…" He waved his hand as if trying to pluck the appropriate word out of the air. "Less ossified. With fewer bureaucrats and Ministry agents always looking over your shoulder."

"I will," I said.

"And see that you stay out of trouble," said Uncle Morgan. "The people in the cities have no morals and no work ethic. Most of them are slugs living on Basic Income. They're barely human these days."

At the time, I had no idea how right he would turn out to be. I really should have listened to Uncle Morgan.

So I called up Mr. Royale, who was delighted with the news. A week later I took the train to Wilson City and began my career as Mr. Royale's errand boy.

Strangely enough, most of my errands involved fixing things. Mr. Royale had a lot of companies, but he rarely hired actual employees since the taxes were so high and the regulations were so complex. Instead, Mr. Royale hired his people as contractors and then paid them on an hourly basis. The pay, I had to admit, was pretty good, but the perks were better. Mr. Royale also paid in "favors", which was why I was able to pay fifty percent below market rent on the micro-apartment I rented, why my mass transit pass was free, and why I had a card that let me buy groceries at ten percent off.

Which was just as well, because Mr. Royale had a lot of work for me to do.

For some reason, he had a hard time finding competent people. Thirty million people lived in Wilson City, most of them in the endless apartment towers surrounding the downtown skyscrapers, so you'd think he could at least find someone who knew the difference between an alternator, a crankshaft, and a rotor, but there weren't that many of them. Sure, Wilson City had a lot of schools… but the people who came out of those schools never seemed to know anything. Like, I was talking to another mechanic, a guy just out of technical school, and he knew all the EcoMin and CareMin regulations backward and forward, but while I was talking to him, I realized he wasn't entirely sure about the difference between voltage and amperage.

I hadn't been to technical school, but I had spent a lot of time with my father between the various mandatory modules of school before the accident, and we had spent almost all our time fixing farm machinery. Dad had also done a sideline fixing cars, so I had spent a lot of time doing that as well. So I knew a lot of different mechanical systems well, which made fixing KwikBreet machines and Mr. Royale's fleet of motor vehicles and cleaning robots pretty easy by comparison.

It turned out that Mr. Royale had trouble finding skilled people because there just weren't that many skilled people in Wilson City.

I started to realize that after my first six weeks or so there. Most of the people I saw in Wilson City were just so… so…

Well, to be blunt, they were *obese*.

I suspected one reason Mr. Royale's cleaning robot rental business did so well because a lot of the citizens of Wilson City were incapable of bending over without injuring themselves. Uncle Morgan had gotten heavier over the last few years, but compared to a lot of people in Wilson City, he was as thin as a whip. Weirdly, the richer people were, the more likely they were to be in shape. I don't know why. Mr. Royale liked to say that once someone had gone on Basic Income, they had no reason to go off it again, and therefore no reason to do anything except eat, drink, vape, and watch videos until they died in their late fifties from diabetes or cirrhosis or cardiac failure, and their bodies went into the organic decompilers to become fertilizers and plastics.

I don't know if he was right or not, but when I went to Basic Housing blocks to repair KwikBreet machines, it seemed like everyone there was obese, even the kids. They spent all their time jacked into the Netrix, living virtual lives in the place of their real ones. Sometimes I thought I could fire a gun over their heads, and they wouldn't notice unless they happened to lose their connection at the same time.

I admit that sometimes I had fantasized about leaving the farm, going to one of the cities, and going on Basic Income and doing whatever I wanted, but after seeing how people in the Basic Housing blocks lived, I swore to myself that I would never, ever end up like that.

So I worked a lot, but I never really relaxed in Wilson City. I didn't fit in. Most of the people my age had never done an honest day's work in their lives, and we didn't have a lot of common ground. Plus, we didn't have the same recreational interests. I liked to actually *do* things—hike and run and go exploring and a good basketball game—did you know you can actually reprogram an autonomous tractor to play horse? I also liked to hunt, but you have to be careful not to let EcoMin find out, so I suppose that wasn't hunting, technically speaking, but poaching.

But no one in Wilson City seemed to like to do *anything*. They were too busy being angels or demons or vampires or pirates in their imaginary worlds. So, when I did have some down time, I mostly spent it with Mr. Royale and his various employees.

"That is exactly the problem, Hammond," he said when I mentioned that to him one day. "No one here likes to do anything. That's why I'm investing in the Safari Company. The Ecology Ministry shut down the last colonization program fifty years ago, and New Princeton has entirely stagnated since then. Man is an explorer! He is a fighter! He needs to build things, and do things, and face dangers, and run risks. He is not made to sit around and wait for cancer or diabetes to kill him off. The people here spend their lives lost in their imaginations because even make-believe challenges are better than none."

I agreed with him, but I didn't know what I could do about it. Going off to start a new colony sounded like a grand adventure, but EcoMin had forbidden any of its citizens to start any such efforts, or even take part in them. It had also scaled back New Princeton's space fleet, on the grounds that Mankind already had too much of a destructive impact on the galactic ecology. So, even joining a scout ship's crew and heading out on a mapping expedition on the edges of the Thousand Worlds was out. Still, I liked mechanical things, and I liked fixing mechanical things, so at least I had plenty to do.

Nevertheless, I was feeling more than a little restless and rebellious when I met Theresa Graff for the first time.

That turned out to be a problem.

I had been in Wilson City for four months, and I was sent to the Central Precinct to fix several malfunctioning KwikBreet machines there. Wilson City's Central Precinct was where all the Acadarchy's Ministries kept their local offices, and the Care Ministry and the Ecology Ministry and the Security Ministry and the Transportation Ministry and all the other government ministries and agencies had buildings there. The larger ones had individual campuses, filled with workers, and after acquiring the contract, no doubt through calling in a few of the favors in which he traded, Mr. Royale installed dozens of KwikBreet machines all around the campuses. Of course, Ministry employees made way more money than Basic Income provided, so they demanded a larger assortment of selections, so the campus machines had more ingredients than the ones installed in the Basic Housing blocks. Consequently, the machines were more complicated, and they broke down more often. I spent a lot of time on one campus or another fixing them.

I had gotten the first four machines fixed, and was on my way to the fifth when I met her. The machine was placed just outside EcoMin's main office, tucked in an alcove between the doors and a towering ten-foot portrait of the current minister, a guy named Paul Valier. The portrait showed Valier wearing a double-breasted black suit as he stood before a radiant jungle, one foot resting upon a rock and one arm flung out as if presenting the jungle to the people of New Princeton. It made him look like a used-car salesman, as if he was announcing a sale on last year's model of electric city cars.

At that moment, however, neither the portrait nor Valier struck me as important. I was wrong about both.

Instead, the sound of someone beating on the KwikBreet machine captured my attention.

"Stupid machine!" shrieked a female voice. "Give me my stupid breet!" She let loose a torrent of furious words, very few of which were printable.

"Why are you hitting my machine?" I said, hurrying forward, my tool bag in my right hand. I had visions of some four-hundred-pound diabetic driving her electric cart into the machine out of pure frustration.

Don't laugh. I'd seen it happen before, and it had taken all afternoon to fix the poor dispenser.

Then the girl hitting the machine turned around, and for a moment my brain froze.

She was, to put it mildly, hot. Hotter than a Spicy Cheese Melt fresh from the nuker.

The sight of her hit me like a thunderbolt. You see, most of the girls I had met since coming to Wilson City were already thirty or forty pounds overweight, which effectively killed any interest I had in asking them out. Theresa, though, Theresa was in shape. She was very fond of yoga, and it showed, especially since it was a warm day and she was wearing nothing more than a tank top and shorts. She had long, thick, black hair, eyes like brilliant sapphires, and full red lips. For a moment, I had a brief vision of grabbing her, pulling her close to me, and kissing her.

Then she started shouting at me and I had to resist the urge to run.

"This is your machine, is it?" she said, stalking forward. She jabbed me in the chest twice with an uncomfortably sharp painted nail. "Then you had better well give me back my money! I paid for a Hummus Vegie Breet with Teriyaki, and I better get it! I…"

I pushed past her in mid-tirade and examined the machine. Pretty or not, maximum volume or not, I had to see if she'd done my machine any damage.

"What are you doing?" she said. I got the idea that people did not often walk past her and ignore her.

"Seeing how much it's going to cost you for punching my machine," I told her.

"What?" she said, her voice going up half an octave.

"You were punching it," I said. "If it's not working, that's probably why."

She folded her arms and glared at me. "Are you saying it's my fault?"

"It isn't mine," I said. "Did you really think that if you scream at it a little more, it'll say sorry and spit out a breet at you?"

To my surprise, she laughed. I had no idea why.

Right there, that was my problem.

It wasn't that I was afraid of girls. Some of Mr. Royale's technicians were so scared of them that they froze up whenever they tried to talk to girls. Me, that wasn't my problem. My problem was that I wasn't scared of them, but I didn't understand them. You might think that isn't a big deal, but then, think about what happens if you're not scared of a chainsaw and you don't understand how it works.

See what I mean? And as girls went, Theresa was the love child of a chainsaw and a hungry shark with a bad temper.

"Okay, maybe I overreacted a little bit," she said. "My blood sugar is like, really low, because I just got done working out, and I was so hungry that I was angry, and I thought one of the vegetarian burritos would be good, but then the stupid machine ate my stupid money so I got really angry."

She somehow said all that with a single breath.

"All right," I said. "If you hang on, I can probably get your money back."

"Really?" she said. "So you can fix these things?"

"It's what I do," I said.

"Fine," she said. "I want to watch."

I shrugged. "Suit yourself." But I was kind of glad for the opportunity to show off a little.

I unlocked the machine and spent a few moments scrutinizing the innards. Fortunately, the malfunction was a simple one—the spindle that wrapped the finished burritos in biodegradable paper had jammed. I kept telling Mr. Royale he ought to buy a better grade of paper, but he explained that saving even one-hundredth of a credit per square foot of wrapping paper added up to tens of thousands of credits per month, so that was that. I fixed the paper spool, ran a diagnostic, and closed the machine up.

"Here you go," I said, handing her five-credit note back. New Princeton's paper money was ugly and garish, all bright purples and blues, and the faces upon the currency changed every year depending upon which historical figures were in political favor at the moment.

"Hey, thanks," she said. "So that really works now?"

"It does," I said. "Anyway, I've got to get going. Have a nice…"

She pushed past me, her shoulder brushing against mine. "I'm still hungry. But if this eats my money again, you owe me five credits." She fed the bill into the machine and punched in her order, and thirty seconds later it spat out a Hummus Veggie KwikBreet, complete with the teriyaki sauce option.

Wrapped properly, I was pleased to note.

She actually squealed in delight and picked up the burrito. "It worked!"

"Uh, yes," I said, edging past her towards the sidewalk. "Enjoy your meal, and…"

"Wait." She grabbed my left forearm. Part of my brain noted that her hand was very soft and very warm. "I'll buy you one too. Only fair, right?"

I had a lot of work to do. I was going to do some work on Mr. Royale's motor pool tonight, and I always enjoyed that. I was alone in the garage at night, and I could blast the music as loud as I wanted with no one to bother me.

On the other hand, I was hungry. And she was pretty.

"All right," I said. "Beef and Shroom with Brown Rice."

"Coming up," she said, feeding another five-credit note into the machine, "since you did such a nice job of fixing the stupid thing." She looked over her shoulder at me. It was a deliberately coquettish look, but she made it work. "My name is Theresa, by the way. Theresa Graff."

"Sam Hammond," I said, extending my hand. She blinked in surprise. People generally didn't shake hands in Wilson City, but the habit had been ingrained young. Theresa laughed and gave my hand a thorough, exaggerated pumping.

"Well, it is a pleasure to meet you, Mr. Sam Hammond," she said. The KwikBreet machine produced my burrito. "Come outside and eat with me."

We sat side-by-side on the curb below one of the towering Ministry buildings. I told her a little about myself, but mostly I listened to her talk and talk and talk. Her mom worked for EcoMin doing some boring job in a boring office, or so she claimed. Her mother had left her father ten years ago, and she had had two stepfathers since, and I could tell she despised both of them, probably because she called the first stepfather Mr. Dumb and the second one Mr. Dumber. She also informed me that she wanted to be a veterinarian because she loved animals, a career I thought unlikely since I could just about imagine her reaction the first time she had to clean out an infection on a cow's backside.

In retrospect, she talked a lot of nonsense, but it wasn't so much that I liked listening to her as I liked watching her while she talked.

"Thanks for dinner," I said, once she paused for breath. "I do need to get back to work."

"Here," she said, thrusting her comm in my direction. "Give me your number."

I shrugged, entered the number, dutifully took hers in return and left. I didn't intend to call her or text her back. She was pretty, and in really good shape, which in Wilson City was as rare as an honest Ministry employee. Yet something about her had just seemed... off. Like, she had been so angry at the KwikBreet machine, so angry that I had thought she might actually try to take a swing at me when I showed up. And she had calmed down disconcertingly fast, so fast that I wondered if something was wrong with her. I may not have had much experience with girls, and I knew women were more emotional than men… but I didn't think they were that much more emotional.

The entire encounter put me in an odd mood. I thought about my parents, what they had been like before the train accident. They had loved each other, as far as I could tell. I thought about what it would be like to get married… and then concluded that I wasn't going to find a quality wife in a place like Wilson City. That, in turn, made me wonder what I was going to do with the rest of my life. I liked fixing machines, but could I do that forever?

On the other hand, so few people in Wilson City seemed to have practical skills that I could probably keep earning a comfortable living until I died, even if I lived to a hundred and twenty. I put the entire thing out of my mind and spent an enjoyable evening fixing some of the cars and vans in Mr. Royale's motor pool, then went home and went to bed.

Theresa texted me the next day, and the day after that, and on the third day, I finally responded. We got together for coffee and started going out regularly.

"That," said Mr. Royale once he realized what was going on, "is an extraordinarily bad idea."

"Why's that?" I said. We were in the central KwikBreet warehouse, where Mr. Royale's fleet of drone-powered vans loaded up with ingredients for the machines and drove out to refill them. I had also taken to repairing the drone vans when they broke down, which happened a lot. New Princeton's standards for automotive manufacture were not high.

"The girl is a hellcat," said Mr. Royale.

"You know her, then?" I said.

"No, but I know her type," said Mr. Royale. "More to the point, I know her mother. Julia Graff is one of the sub-ministers in the Ecology Ministry."

I blinked in surprise. "Really. She said her mom had some boring job in one of the Ministries, but I didn't realize that."

"Her job is many things, but boring is not one of them," said Mr. Royale. "She started out as a secretary, and now is running one of the ministry's interior departments. Along the way, she married and divorced three ministry officials, one of whom committed suicide, one of whom is in prison, and the third of whom was demoted and reassigned to a waste processing plant in the desert."

"Yeah," I said. "Theresa didn't mention that."

"Ms. Graff is a very dangerous and ruthless woman," said Mr. Royale, "and she can call on more favors than I can. Let's be honest, Sam. A girl raised by a mother like that? She won't be particularly stable. Best to stay as far away from her as possible."

"Uh," I said. "Yeah." My brain knew that he was right. The rest of my body was thinking about how she looked.

Mr. Royale sighed. "Just don't do anything stupid, and if you do something stupid, don't get caught." He hesitated for a moment, and to my surprise he seemed slightly embarrassed. "Ah... you do know, how shall we say, the facts of life..."

"I grew up on a farm," I said.

"Right," said Mr. Royale. "Just be careful. Good mechanics are hard to find, and I don't want her to send you to prison."

I should have listened.

Theresa, like me, didn't have many friends. I wasn't sure why, and then I realized it was because she also liked to do things. Too many of the kids our age in Wilson City were lost in the

Netrix and most of them were eager to get on Basic Income as soon as possible. Theresa, on the other hand, was full of life. She loved to go running. I wasn't in bad shape, but I still found it a challenge to keep up with her. She liked to drive fast too, and she was delighted when I showed her how to override the speed controls on the car her mom had bought her. She had energy, so much energy that it seemed to explode out of her, which is why she found Wilson City as intolerable as I did.

But every now and then, her mood changed.

She was prone to black, vicious depressions, and when a dark mood came upon her, anything would set her off. When she was depressed, she liked to break things—throwing bottles against the wall and the like. She also had a vaping habit that her mom didn't know about, and when she vaped stoke, one of the city's more popular mind-benders, she liked company.

In hindsight, Theresa Graff was an international parade of red flags. I was too young and stupid to realize it, though.

I was in what I thought was love, and I was an idiot, and I proved how deep the idiocy went on the night we got stoked and got our hands on some spray paint.

It was a Friday night about seven months after Mr. Royale had hired me. It had been a long day, and I had done repairs on nineteen different KwikBreet machines scattered around Wilson City. Theresa, too, had had a long day, though I suspect her day had been more boring than difficult. At her mother's insistence, Theresa was attending Wilson City University on a full scholarship that had been arranged by her mother for a degree in ecological justice. The problem was that she had absolutely no interest in eco-justice.

"It's awful!" she said with disgust. We had met at the WCU campus after I had finished, and somehow she had already gotten a box of stoke from somewhere, so we sat drinking in my car. The sun had set twenty minutes ago, and I was on my third vape, but she was on her fourth. "It is so boring! And Mom knows all the professors, so I can't even skip class. If I don't show up, they email her and she sends her assistant around to give me a lecture about responsibility and all that!" Her voice went up an octave on the last word. "I feel like I'm in prison. It makes me just want to scream!"

I laughed.

"What is so funny, Samuel Hammond?" she demanded.

"Your voice," I said. "It gets higher when you get angry." I did my best falsetto imitation of her. "I just want to scream!"

She glared at me. "You're not nearly as funny as you think you are!"

I just laughed harder.

"What now?" Theresa demanded.

"You did it again," I said.

"It did not," she said. "It… oh, it did, didn't it?" She burst out into a long, wild laugh, and slapped the dashboard of my car. "I did it again! It's probably funny because I'm stoked."

"Probably," I said, opening another canister to load the vape, which was out.

"But, Sam, it's so boring," said Theresa. "You can't imagine. The professors do not shut up. Not ever! All they ever do is talk about ecology and the environment and how we need to stay out of space to preserve the interstellar environment, as if there is anything out there anyhow." She somehow got the words out without slowing them—inebriation just made her talk even faster. "I just want to go out and do stuff, you know? Not just sit around and listen to fat old morons talking at me all day."

"Then you should quit school and get a job," I said, gesturing with the now-loaded vape. "You know? You should learn to fix KwikBreet machines. You'd never be bored again."

Her nose crinkled with disgust. "That's stupid. I don't want to be as boring as you."

Something inside me snarled at the remark.

"You think I'm boring?" I said.

"Well, all you ever do is work, and talk about work," said Theresa. "You might be more fun if you went on Basic Income and had more time for stuff."

"I'm not boring," I said.

"You totally are," said Theresa. "All you ever talk about is work."

"I do not," I said. I couldn't decide if I wanted to be angry or not, in a drunken sort of way. It helped that when I drank too much I tended to find everything hilarious, even stupid stuff, and it took a lot to get angry through the buzz in my head. "I just work a lot. I mean, would you rather hang out with some fat loaf on Basic?"

"No," said Theresa. "But you could have some fun. I mean, you're going to be rich someday?"

"What?" I said.

"I can tell," said Theresa. She leaned forward, wobbled a bit, and tapped me on the nose a few times. "I. Can. Always. Tell. See, babe, you're too restless. Too much energy. A guy like you, you'd never be happy to just sit around the way everyone else does."

"It's hard to find things to do," I said. "Mr. Royale says so. There are too many laws. Too many regulations. No one can do anything because of EcoMin and CareMin and SafeMin!"

Theresa scowled. I expected her to take umbrage at the insults to her mother's ministry, but she nodded instead, her hair flopping around her head.

"I hate EcoMin!" she said. "I am so tired of hearing about it! My mom never shuts up about it, and all the stupid professors never shut up about it, and I just want them all to shut up and stop talking all the time!"

"Yes!" I said, gesturing with the vape. "We can't do anything. Mr. Royale makes money, but he has to jump through a billion hoops and call in a billion favors to do anything. If we didn't have the ministries breathing down our necks, we'd be... we'd be..."

"Richer?" said Theresa.

"That," I said, nodding forcefully. It was just as well that I was sitting, because if I had nodded that hard while standing up, I would have fallen over. "That is it. We'd all be better off without those jerks."

"We should show them," said Theresa. "Someone was spraying a bunch of graffiti all over campus. We should show EcoMin just what we think of them."

That was a terrible idea.

"That is a brilliant idea!" I said, handing the vape to her. "Car!" I whacked the dashboard a few times, and the car's automated system turned itself on. "Drive us to the hardware store. One that's, you know, open at..."

"One in the morning," said Theresa.

"Yeah, what she said." I tapped the dashboard. "Hardware store."

"Proceeding to destination," announced the car in a calm voice. I preferred to drive the thing myself, but even in my impaired state, I had enough wit left to realize that driving while highly stoked was a terrible idea.

The car's computer took us to an all-night charging station and convenience store that also happened to sell some home repair stuff. I bought a dozen cans of red spray paint from the indifferent middle-aged man behind the counter and wobbled back out to my car. Theresa grinned as I passed her the bag, the cans clanking against each other.

"Where should we go?" I said.

"Where do you think?" said Theresa, her eyes wide, her cheeks flushed. I don't think she had ever looked quite so beautiful, but I have to admit her eyes looked more than a little crazy.

"Yeah," I said, and we both turned to the dashboard and shouted in unison. "EcoMin!"

"I'm sorry. Could you please repeat that?" announced the computer.

Theresa indicated a destination that was improbable, unless computers have souls.

"The Ecology Ministry," I said, enunciating carefully. That time the computer parsed the words and the car shifted into motion.

A short time later the car stopped in front of EcoMin's sprawling campus in the heart of Wilson City. I loaded another cartridge and took another hit as the car drove, which seemed like an excellent idea at the time, though my head was starting to whirl. The car's computer parked on the curb of the Ministry's main drive, next to the giant concrete sign with the EcoMinlogo and a picture of Paul Valier standing before a forest, showing his teeth.

"Doesn't it look stupid?" said Theresa, jabbing her finger at the window.

"Let's fix that!" I said, throwing open the car door. I grabbed two cans of spray paint, surged to my feet, overbalanced, and landed flat on my face.

Theresa burst out laughing, leaning on the car. I glared at her, then saw the humor of the situation, and then started laughing myself.

Then we staggered to the EcoMin sign and began engaging in an act of what was subsequently termed "politically motivated antiplanetary public vandalism."

We started with the portrait of Minister Paul Valier, giving him first a mustache, then devil horns, and then a variety of other enhancements, each more anatomically improbable than the last. After that, we moved on to the EcoMin sign itself, scribbling layers of spray paint over it. In short order, we used up all twelve cans of red spray paint. As I walked back and forth to the car to get new cans, I got dizzier and dizzier, until it felt like a good idea to sit down on the cool, damp grass.

That felt really nice, so I lay down, which felt even nicer. The stars spun overhead, faster and faster. Were they supposed to do that? I couldn't remember the stars spinning before.

I thought I heard something. It sounded like Theresa driving away in my car. But I was too out of it to care.

I woke up the next morning with a stupendous headache, a mouth that felt like it had been lined with dry cotton, and eight scowling officers wearing the black-and-white uniform of the Security Ministry staring down at me.

"Um," I said. There really wasn't any point in denying it, not when a dozen empty cans of spray paint lay around me, and

I had gotten the stuff on my hands and pants. Spray painting while stoked is not a great recipe for accuracy.

One of the officers produced my wallet. "Samuel Hammond?"

"Uh," I said. "Yeah."

"You are under arrest for vandalism of Acadarchy property, trespassing on Ecology Ministry property, public intoxication, illegal dissent…"

The list of charges went on from there.

My trial was the next day. The Acadarchy is slow about a lot of things, but exacting fines and punishments isn't one of them. I sat in the defendant's box in a wood-paneled LawMin courtroom. Theresa was the first witness, and she broke down sobbing as she described how I had forced her to drink alcohol, taken her on a wild ride through the city, and threatened her when she would not join in my anti-Acadarchy hooliganism.

I wasn't all that surprised. Disappointed, sure. But not exactly shocked. I had pretty much known what kind of girl she was from the moment we had met, after all.

Julia Graff was the next witness. She looked a great deal like Theresa, albeit with thirty additional years, forty extra pounds, and a flat, cold-eyed stare that reminded me of a reptile. She testified how she had warned me away from her daughter, how she had urged Theresa to stay away from me. All lies, of course, but I suppose when you are a sub-minister, perjury is not such a big deal.

Mr. Royale testified in my defense, citing my excellent work record and diligence, arguing that as a country boy new to the big city, I had been overwhelmed by the temptations of drink and loose women. Julia Graff glared at him, and I felt bad for him that he had made a powerful new enemy on my behalf.

In the end, the judge was inclined towards leniency. I was given the choice between a year in prison and a year of community service, to be decided at the discretion of the court. I chose the latter, of course, and after Mr. Royale arranged a discreet bribe to the judge, my service year was assigned to him.

In retrospect, I should have picked prison. It would have been *considerably* safer. But at the time, I was just glad not to be behind bars.

Mr. Royale drove me back to the motor pool after the trial.

"I owe you, sir," I told him. "Big time."

"Well," said Mr. Royale. "I won't pretend that little arrangement wasn't costly. But there are few pleasures in life as exquisite as saying 'I told you so'... and I did warn you about that girl."

I looked out the window for a while. "Yeah. I should have listened to you. But thanks anyway."

We rode in silence for a while.

"So I suppose I spend the next year fixing things for free?" I said.

"Not quite," said Mr. Royale. "I have something else in mind. Specifically, the reason I hired you."

"To fix machines?" I said. I was tired from the last few days, and my head still hurt.

"Not quite," said Mr. Royale. "Do you remember what caught my attention on the day we met?"

I thought for a minute. "Almost getting eaten by fangwolves."

"That does have a way of focusing the mind, yes," said Mr. Royale, "but that's not quite it. No, what caught my attention was how effectively you dealt with the fangwolves."

I shrugged. "You shoot them if they come after you. That's all there is to it. Out in the countryside it's a bad idea to go anywhere alone and without a gun."

"That's just it," said Mr. Royale. "Don't you see, Hammond? I am no intellectual, but I am not a stupid man. Yet I didn't know I was in mortal danger! I blundered along and nearly got myself killed because I didn't know what you did. Not many people on New Princeton have your particular sort of knowledge. Too many of us live in cities. A fangwolf might as well be a creature from another planet. You see, I didn't recruit you to fix food dispensers. I recruited you because I wanted to hire you for the Safari Company."

"The Safari Company?" I said, sorting through my memory. Mr. Royale had a lot of fingers in a lot of different pies, and it took me a minute to recall that particular pie. "The hunting company out in the Arborea system?"

"I'm a major investor," said Mr. Royale, "and I wanted you for the Company because I think you would be an excellent fit."

"You didn't strike me as much of a hunter, sir," I said.

"I'm not," said Mr. Royale. "I have no objection to it, simply no interest in it. But I think that running the Safari Company is the best hope we have of renewing interest in space colonization." He shook his head. "You've seen our society. It is completely and utterly stagnant, and growing a little more corrupt and a little more stagnant with every passing year. I just bribed a judge. I shouldn't be able to do that, but I do so regularly." He tapped the wheel for a moment. "You know there are a hundred different habitable systems within hyperspace range from New Princeton?"

"I didn't know that," I said.

"It's not widely publicized," said Mr. Royale. "The Ecology Ministry forbids all colonization on habitable worlds for fear of damaging their environments. Asteroid mining and stations on lifeless worlds are well and good, but we need to grow and expand. And I hope… well, it is my hope that the Safari Company might change that. That if enough rich and prominent citizens get out and see another world, we might change their attitudes, and perhaps start founding new colonies again."

He drove in silence for a moment.

"That sounds like a worthwhile goal, sir," I said. "I would like to be a part of it. Which is just as well, since I don't have much choice in the matter."

Mr. Royale laughed. "I appreciate a man with a firm grasp of the facts. You leave for Arborea tomorrow with another of my employees, a man named Winston Tanner. He knows his business, and I want you to assist him however he sees fit."

"What are we supposed to do?" I said.

"Two things," said Mr. Royale. "First, make sure the Safari Company is a success. Second, investigate any irregularities, because there have been a lot of questionable irregularities. I suspect one of the other investors is trying to sabotage the project."

"I will, sir," I said.

At the time, I was pretty excited. A new world! I had never thought I would leave New Princeton, but the prospect of traveling to another planet was exciting.

Though if I had known how much trouble there was on Arborea, maybe I would have stayed on New Princeton.

Chapter 2

Environmentalism for Fun and Profit

First, I had to get my shots. Arborea had a wide variety of microorganisms and viruses, all of which regarded humans the same way Theresa viewed a vegetarian KwikBreet when she was ravenous. Mr. Royale sent me to the nearest clinic, and a doctor pumped me full of a dozen shots and made me swallow three or four handfuls of pills. I spent the rest of the day feverish and sweating, but once the side effects wore off, I was supposed to be immune to the various diseases spawned in Arborea's jungles.

That was the theory, anyhow.

The next day I took a taxi to Wilson City's spaceport and met Winston Tanner for the first time.

Tanner was waiting for me in the observation lounge. He was middle-aged and bald, with an impressive beer gut, but he had arms as thick as my legs, and the hard expression I had come to associate with men who had left the Security Ministry for more lucrative employment in the field of private practice. When I met him, he was cracking walnuts with one hand, popping the nut into his mouth and tucking the shards of the shell away into a waste bag.

He looked up as I approached. "You're the kid with the spray paint?"

"Um," I said. "Yes. My name's Sam Hammond. You must be Mr. Tanner?"

"Just Tanner," he said, finishing off his last walnut and getting to his feet. We shook hands, and I had the suspicion he could have crushed my hand like one of those walnuts shells if he had felt like it. "You've got your stuff?"

"Yes, sir," I said. Everything I needed was in my backpack and a wheeled suitcase.

"Right," said Tanner, grabbing his own bags. "We're taking a shuttle to the orbital platform, and then a warp liner out to Arborea. Let's get a move on, Spraycan."

It seemed I had just acquired a nickname. I can't say I was enthusiastic about it, but it could have been worse. And I couldn't pretend I hadn't earned it.

We checked in the counter, presented our tickets, and boarded the shuttle, and a few minutes later I had my first experience with spaceflight.

I confess I did not care for it. As I kid I had from time to time thought about joining a merchant ship, flying the circuits between the various colony worlds founded by the scores of human governments scattered across the galaxy, as not all the governments were as restrictive with their colonization policies, but there were so many legal hoops and requirements that I abandoned the idea. Plus, as it happens, taking off hurts. The shuttle lifted off with a roar, the acceleration pressing me into my seat, and for a few moments, I thought I would explode like a tomato squished beneath a car wheel.

It did get more pleasant once we got loose of New Princeton's gravity well and into orbit, allowing the shuttle's artificial gravity systems to compensate for inertia and generate an illusion of planetary gravity. I gaped wide-eyed at the curvature of the planet, at the green continents and blue oceans and white clouds. It was so huge! Wilson City and Uncle Morgan's farm had been my entire world, and I had thought Wilson City vast beyond reckoning.

On the face of New Princeton, Wilson City was just a glowing smudge… and even New Princeton was just one world among thousands.

"It's so little," I heard myself.

"Yup," said Tanner, not looking up from his reader. He was reading a magazine about hunting firearms. Most of the article seemed to feature a bikini-clad woman holding the hunting rifle in question.

"I mean… I never realized it was so big out here," I said. I realized that sounded lame, so I decided to stop talking.

For the first time, Tanner looked up from his reader. "First time up here?"

I nodded.

Tanner grunted. "Well, I told Mr. Royale to find me a farm kid for this business and looks like he came through. Have you ever been off the farm before?"

"I lived in Wilson City for a while," I said.

"Right," said Tanner. "Wilson City. If that isn't the big bad universe, than nothing is." It took me a minute to detect the sarcasm. "Still, the entire planet of Arborea has as much people as maybe one Basic Income housing block in Wilson City. So long as you can handle yourself outdoors, you'll be up for the job."

"About that," I said. "What exactly will we be doing?"

Tanner grunted. "My title is Security Director. That means I'm responsible for all forms of security. Yours is Indentured Worker to the Security Director, which means you do what I tell you, make yourself useful, and don't get yourself eaten by a tromosaur."

"Tromosaur?" I said. "What is a tromosaur?"

"Apex predator in Arborea," said Tanner. "One of them, anyway. Don't worry. You'll find out soon enough, assuming you don't get eaten."

That was not a reassuring thought.

"Can I ask another question?" I said.

Tanner nodded, not impatient, but not exactly interested, either.

"What does Mr. Royale want us to do?" I said.

Tanner considered that for a moment. "He's a major investor in the Safari Company, but he's not the only one."

"He mentioned some internal issues. Is that a form of security?"

"Yeah. Our main objective, whatever our official responsibilities might be," said Tanner, "is to make sure that the Company isn't sabotaged from within. We're going to check into irregularities and things like that. Make sure that Mr. Royale doesn't waste his money." He tapped his reader to turn the page, revealing an article topped by an image of a woman in a very small swimsuit holding a very large gun. "But this isn't the place to talk about it. We'll discuss it more later."

With that, he returned his attention to his reader.

It was a four-hour flight to the orbital station. We disembarked from the shuttle, and I looked around with wide eyes at everything. The station was shaped like a big metal doughnut, with concourses across its circumference. The concourses themselves looked kind of like a combination of a dock yard, a cargo bay, and a shopping mall. Thousands of people went about their business, and I even saw my first aliens, creatures that looked vaguely like ambulatory humanoid elephants. Evidently, they came from a star system a long distance away and traded rare ore for certain forms of fungus that only grew upon New Princeton.

Tanner and I then boarded a starliner, a hyperspace-capable passenger ship called the *Kennedy*. The ship had dozens of luxurious staterooms, opulent restaurants, and even a casino with card tables. Alas, Mr. Royale did not believe in such extravagances, so Tanner and I shared a cabin in third class. At least it was clean, thanks to the ship's housekeeping drones.

An hour later, the *Kennedy* activated its hyperdrive, setting out on the circuit of a hundred worlds it covered, and I learned something unpleasant about myself.

"Ah, don't worry about it," said Tanner, clapping me on the back once I had finished throwing up the last of my breakfast into the toilet. "The first jump is tricky for everyone. Could be worse. I knew a guy who crapped himself in front of his fiancée the first time he was on a ship that went to hyperdrive."

"Thanks so much," I croaked, rummaging through the basket of complimentary toiletries to find some mouthwash.

"Take these," said Tanner, lifting a little vial of pills from the basket. He slapped a memory card next to the pills. "Then start reading these. It'll help get you up to speed on Safari Company and Outpost Town."

"Outpost Town?" I said.

"The Company's headquarters on Arborea," said Tanner.

I had hoped to explore the ship, at least the third-class portions of it, but my stomach did not agree with hyperspace travel at all and I felt terrible. So instead I camped out in my bunk, plugged Tanner's memory card into my reader, and read up on Safari Company and its operations on Arborea. To my surprise, all the manuals were actually useful. I had read enough tractor and engine manuals to realize that not all technical writers were created equal, but whoever had written Safari Company's manuals had done a good job.

So when the *Kennedy* exited hyperspace above Arborea we rode the shuttle down to Outpost Town, I wasn't completely disoriented.

Arborea looked… well, from orbit, Arborea looked amazing.

It didn't look anything like New Princeton. Arborea looked mostly green from orbit, with white at the polar ice caps. The green of the continents was a harsh color. The seas were mostly green as well, though they faded to blue at the center. According to the manuals, the green came from the algae that grew in the waters, algae that supported a wide variety of sea life. The Safari Company let more enterprising guests rent boats to go fishing, though this was dangerous because some of the sea creatures could swallow the boats in one gulp.

That is one thing I should mention about Arborea. I had never heard the term "megafauna" before reading the manuals, but that was an accurate description of many of the native species on Arborea. It means "really, really big animals." When Mr. Royale had described the Safari Company to me, I had a mental picture of a bunch of rich guys getting in a jeep, driving out in the countryside of New Princeton, and shooting fangwolves.

It had never occurred to me that some of the predators on Arborea would make fangwolves look like cuddly little puppies.

We rode the shuttle down from the *Kennedy* to Outpost Town on Arborea's central continent, which did not as yet have an official name. I noticed that most of our fellow passengers appeared to be wealthy, possibly wealthy enough to afford their own suites in first-class. After that, I stopped paying attention to the passengers because my stomach did not approve of atmospheric reentry. I took some pills that Tanner gave me and closed my eyes until the nausea passed.

"I told Mr. Royale to find me a farm kid," said Tanner, "and he came through." For the first time since leaving New Princeton, he sounded amused. "You're such a farm kid that you don't like to fly at all."

"Flying's fine," I said, the shuttle shuddering with reentry, fire flaring past the windows. "I don't mind it. Now if you can convince my stomach of that…"

Fortunately, our flight soon leveled out, the pilot switching on the antigrav drive, and I watched through the windows as we flew over miles of vivid green jungle until Outpost Town came into sight.

It looked… well, it looked like an expensive resort.

It was laid out like a little town, with the main street lined with hotels, restaurants, and fancy shops. Behind the hotels, discreetly out of sight, were lower, blockier buildings that housed the staff quarters and the offices and the mechanical plants. One side of Outpost Town faced the green waters of the ocean, though with the microflora count in those waters, no one in their right mind would want to swim in it. The rest of the town faced the jungle, and the trees and the plants had been cut down for a half mile in every direction. At the edge of the cleared land stood a fence of black posts topped with sonic alarms every thirty yards. From what I had read, the tromosaurs hated ultra high-frequency noises, and so the sonic alarms emitted a constant whistle inaudible to human ears. If a tromosaur pack tried to breach the fence, the sonic alarms would increase in volume and radio back to Outpost Town, and a security team would go out in a hurry.

I wondered if the tromosaurs were really that dangerous.

Our shuttle touched down on the landing pad, and the rich passengers got out first. Tanner and I gathered our bags and disembarked after them. A small army of sleek white service drones manufactured to look vaguely like women attended to the passengers. The part of my brain devoted to mechanics pointed out how inefficient using two legs was for robotic loco-motion. A set of treads would really have been more efficient, though it would have ruined the aesthetic. Another part of my brain noticed that it was much hotter and humid than on New Princeton, and I probably wouldn't need the coats I had packed.

The rest of my brain noticed the pretty woman heading towards us.

She was somewhere in her thirties, and even though she was wearing a loose blue jumpsuit, I could tell that she was in good shape. She had long coppery red hair tied back in a tail and bright blue eyes and a wide smile went over her face as she saw Tanner.

"Winston!" she said, and for the first time, I saw Tanner smile. He dropped his bags and swallowed her in a hug. "You were gone too long."

"The problems of business, my dear," said Tanner. "You know how Mr. Royale likes to talk."

"The only thing he likes more than talking is making money," said the woman. Her eyes shifted to me. "He sent you that assistant?"

"He did," said Tanner. "Sam Hammond, this is my wife, Kayla."

She smiled at me, and my brain froze up a little. Fortunately, my mother had been a fanatic about drilling proper manners into me, and I was grateful to fall back on them now.

I wished I could have thanked her for that.

"Ma'am," I said, sticking out my right hand. "It's a pleasure to meet you, Mrs. Tanner."

Kayla shook my hand. "Likewise. You can call me Kayla."

I saw Tanner staring at me. Suddenly I remembered him crushing those walnuts in the spaceport, and I had a brief vision of him doing the exact same thing to my head.

"Yes, Mrs. Tanner," I said.

Kayla laughed, and Tanner nodded approvingly.

"Well, Mr. Hammond, I hope you are helpful to my husband," said Kayla. "We have a lot of work to do here, and not enough hands for it all."

"Yes, Mrs. Tanner," I said. That seemed like a safe answer.

"Hoskins wanted to see you right away," said Kayla.

Tanner groaned. "I suppose he wants to complain."

"Now, now," said Kayla, slipping her arm through his. "He's good at his job."

"Fine," said Tanner. "I'll talk to him. And then I'm spending the rest of the day with you." He gestured at me. "Come on, Spraycan. We'll find something useful for you to do. You can start by carrying our bags."

Tanner's stuff was heavy, but it was a lot better than spending time in prison for something as stupid as vandalizing Acadarchy property, so I didn't complain. I suppose in the distant past men made stirring speeches when stepping upon a new world for the first time. I spent my first moments on a new world dragging Tanner's baggage behind me while he discussed dinner with his wife. We stopped by Tanner's suite in the staff barracks to drop off Kayla and Tanner's bags, and then I followed Tanner to the administrative building.

Despite Outpost Town's outer glitz and shine, there was a lot of work still to be done. I saw bundles of wires hanging from the ceiling here and there, or walls pulled aside to reveal ductwork and conduits. All the buildings were the sort of cheap prefab stuff that the automated factories on New Princeton could turn out in a hurry.

Tanner turned a corner, and we stepped into a small office. A half-dozen computer monitors sat on the office's L-shaped desk, and stacks of paper covered the rest of its surface. A bug zapper hung from the ceiling in the corner, drawing odd green-shelled insects with twelve legs. At the desk sat a fat man in a short-sleeved shirt, bald and red-faced, his expression a massive scowl as he glared at a monitor displaying a spreadsheet.

"Hoskins?" said Tanner. "Kayla said you wanted to see me."

"Ah!" said Hoskins, heaving himself to his feet with a grunt. "You're back! How was the trip?"

"Uneventful enough," said Tanner. "Royale and the other investors are on board, so we'll have time yet."

"Good," said Hoskins, producing a soiled handkerchief and mopping his brow. "The construction is having trouble hitting dates. This is the sixth time we've had to revise the schedule." He seemed to see me for the first time. "Who's this?"

"Tom Hoskins, meet Sam Hammond, my new deputy," said Tanner. "Royale insisted." Hoskins stuck out his hand, and I shook it. "Best part is he's indentured for eighteen months, so we just have to feed him. We don't have to pay him."

"Splendid," said Hoskins. His eyes narrowed. "Why are you indentured?"

"Nothing very exciting," I told him. "I spray-painted a sign on the EcoMin campus."

Hoskins blinked, and then laughed. "Ha! I heard about that! That was funny. Stupid, but funny." He clapped Tanner on the shoulder, circled his desk, and sat back down with a sigh. "Don't try that here. Else Mr. Charles will have a word with you."

Tanner groaned. "That lunatic is still here?"

"He's Chief Guide now," said Hoskins. "He's a little peculiar, but he's very good at his job. Anyway, I've got bigger problems. That load of construction drones? Defective, the lot of them. No one's qualified to fix them, and New Princeton Robotics refuses to honor the warranty…"

Tanner grunted, and then jerked a thumb at me. "The kid's supposed to be pretty good with mechanical stuff."

"You are?" said Hoskins, heaving himself out of his seat again. "Then follow me."

I started to follow him, but Tanner caught my arm.

"Keep a careful eye out," he said in a quiet voice. "Watch for anything unusual."

And that was my introduction to life at Outpost Town.

I spent the rest of the day and a good chunk of the night fixing the construction drones. There were twenty-five of the things, big boxy yellow drones with treads and a rotating turret on their back that held a variety of earth-moving tools. I had spent most of my childhood and teenage years helping first my father and then Uncle Morgan fix autonomous tractors, and these things were no different. As it happened, it was an easy fix. Someone had disconnected the computer core from the engine on every single drone, so I just had to re-solder the connections and restart the drones. Uncle Morgan's tractors suffered that breakdown due to jostling, but someone had deliberately broken the connection in the construction drones.

I might not have been the brightest guy in the universe, as my little misadventure with Theresa proved, but even I recognized sabotage when I saw it.

And there was a lot of sabotage at Outpost Town.

Tanner later told me that he had a theory there were two rival factions at war inside EcoMin. One wanted to see Safari Company and Outpost Town fail. This faction did things like sabotage the construction drones, load defective software on the computers, misplace shipping schedules, lose paperwork, and so forth. It seemed this faction wasn't quite powerful enough to hit Safari Company with crippling fines and put it out of business, but EcoMin had enough power that individual members within it could easily cause all kind of trouble.

The second faction, the more powerful faction, wanted to see the Safari Company succeed, and it was easy to see why.

It turned out that really rich people from throughout the Thousand Worlds were willing to pay enormous sums of money for the privilege of hunting alien game.

Hunting on New Princeton was one thing. Humans had lived there for fifteen hundred years and the ecosystem had been more or less tamed. As I read through the Company's files, I found that as mankind had spread into the Thousand Worlds and founded colonies, there had been no less than five colonization attempts upon Arborea. The first attempt had failed due to lack of funds, and the second had failed because of political strife among the colonists.

The remaining three efforts had failed when Arborea's predators had eaten every single one of the colonists.

Because of some combination of the atmosphere, the vegetation, and the distance from the local star, Arborea hosted enormous, well-armored herbivores and vicious, deadly predators. Hunting a fangwolf on New Princeton might get you killed. Hunting a tankstrider or a platewhale or one of the other huge herbivores that roamed the jungles required helicopters, heavy explosives, and tactical expertise, and an angry tankstrider could probably trample Outpost Town into dust.

EcoMin controlled the hunting permits on Arborea, and the permit to hunt a tankstrider was twenty million credits. Twenty million! And that was one of the cheaper ones. The permit for a platewhale was fifty million, and the pay scale just went up for the larger animals. EcoMin was making money hand over fist from Safari Town, and I guess if the average official had to choose between preserving planetary ecologies and a raise, most of them would choose a raise. The Safari Company also made money hand over fist, even though the ministry took two-thirds of the license fee. Of course, there were other ways to make money—the restaurants, the souvenir shops, the luxury hotels, the high-end guns and ammunition, the personal helicopters and hunting guides, and all the other services Outpost Town offered.

Mr. Royale might have suffered any number of business failures, but this time, it seemed like he had picked a winner. It also helped that Safari Company didn't have to worry about lawsuits since every guest had to sign a mountain of paperwork indemnifying both Safari Company and EcoMin from every possible form of liability.

The reason for that was made quite clear to me by Senior Guide Hiram Charles.

Tanner might have been Director of Security, which meant he was in charge of security within Outpost Town and the perimeter of the sonic fence. As Senior Guide, Charles was responsible for overseeing the hunting trips into the jungle and managing the guides, and he took this very seriously.

Though to be fair, I think there wasn't a subject under the sun that Charles didn't take seriously.

"What is the number one killer of Safari Company employees and guests?" demanded Charles during the first hour of my mandatory three-day training session with him.

He glared at me. This was intimidating, but Hiram Charles glared at everyone. He was a short, blocky man, with lots of muscle, close-cropped black hair, and features that looked as if at least one of his grandparents had been descended from one or another of the Asian nations that scattered across the Thousand Worlds after the discovery of the hyperdrive. I had never seen him wear anything but combat fatigues and body armor, and I suspected he slept in them.

"The tromosaurs, sir?" I said. The tromosaurs were dangerous. The tankstriders and the platewhales and the other herbivores generally ignored humans unless they were provoked, and when provoked they could bring down helicopters and wipe out an entire hunting party. The tromosaurs, on the other hand, actively hunted humans. They didn't fear us in the slightest, and almost always shadowed hunting parties. I suppose compared to an armored tankstrider, humans had to be a lot less work to kill.

"No!" barked Charles. "The tromosaurs are deadly, yes, but there is a deadlier foe by far." He paced back and forth at the front of the conference room, his shadow flickering across the wall as he stepped into the projector's field. "Can you guess it, Indentured Worker Hammond?"

He always called me that. It would have been weird, except he called everyone by their title—Security Director Tanner, Managing Director Hoskins, Technical Writer, Pilot, & Assistant Business Manager Kayla Tanner, and so forth. Sometimes I wondered how he could get through an entire sentence without running out of oxygen.

"No, sir," I said.

"Inattention!" said Charles. "That is the deadliest foe of all. Arborea is an unforgiving world, and she repays inattention with death. Constant awareness, Indentured Worker Hammond, constant awareness! These must be our watchwords."

With that, Charles decreed that I was ready and would accompany him on a hunting party tomorrow.

"You'll be fine," said Kayla when I told Tanner about it.

Kayla Tanner had taken me under her wing, much to her husband's bemusement. The Tanners didn't have any children. I never worked up the courage to ask why not, but I suspected there was some sort of genetic problem. I would have thought my criminal past would have put off Mrs. Tanner, but she didn't seem to care. Based on what I heard, she was the oldest daughter of a farm family on New Princeton and had gotten her start in piloting by flying her father's crop dusters, so she would have seen the hard hand of EcoMin on a regular basis. And since she'd been the oldest, she was used to telling younger people what to do.

She could cook too. Mr. Royale's KwikBreets are well and good, but there's no substitute for a good home-cooked meal.

"Hiram knows what he's doing," said Kayla, setting a pot of stew upon the table and seating herself. I sat across from her and Tanner, and I didn't eat until Tanner and Kayla had served themselves. I was always on my best behavior at these dinners, partly out of gratitude, and partly because I was still a little frightened of Tanner.

"The man's an obsessive," said Tanner.

"Maybe," conceded Kayla. "Probably. But he's very good at his job. Listen to him, follow his lead, and you'll be fine."

"Remember," said Tanner, pointing a thick finger at me, "always watch out for tromosaurs."

I nodded. "Watch for the telltale ripples, if I see one, assume there are two others that I can't see, keep my sonic alarm ready at all times, and if cornered do not let them get me down on the ground."

"See?" said Kayla. "You'll do fine."

Tanner grunted. "I give you a fifty-fifty chance."

I was a little unsettled, but Kayla laughed, so I decided he was kidding. Maybe.

The next morning I flew out with Charles's hunting party, escorting a Safari Company client named Lucius Rogson.

He was the single most annoying man I had ever met in my entire life.

Lucius Rogson was a short, somewhat doughy fellow, and insisted on dressing in expensive double-breasted business suits despite the fact that Arborea's climate made him sweat through both shirt and jacket in about five minutes. He had a habit of asking questions of everything, which Charles was happy to answer, seeing them as demonstrating a valuable quality of diligence. Unfortunately, Rogson invariably misinterpreted the answers, reached erroneous conclusions, and ran with them. Apparently, Rogson was the finance director for some massive interplanetary corporation or another, and after watching him attempt to put on his own body armor, I decided then and there that if I ever came into money, I would never invest any of it with his company.

Rogson had two aides that were almost as annoying as he was—a prim, tight-lipped lawyer type in a suit who looked like he had a running spreadsheet of deductible expenses in his head, and a burly ex-Security Ministry guy like Tanner. Unlike Tanner, Rogson's bodyguard put on a big show of carrying expensive weapons around on his belt, and while I was no expert on military hardware, I knew just enough to realize that his pistols looked scarier than they really were. They had a lot more chrome and attachments than were strictly necessary.

We took one of the Company's quadcopters and flew off into the jungle. I wondered why the Company just didn't use antigrav-equipped transports for hunting expeditions, but evidently, some kind of fungal spore in the jungle played havoc on antigrav engines. The quadcopters were safer and cheaper anyway. The particular quadcopter we used looked sleek and deadly, its four rotors housed in metal rings jutting from the fuselage. A pair of large-caliber chin guns jutted from beneath the pilot's canopy.

The quadcopter carried Rogson and his two assistants, who in my head I had dubbed the Lawyer and the Bodyguard. The pilot sat alone in the cockpit, while Charles and four of his guides sat with Rogson and his assistants in the passenger compartment. I sat next to Charles, shifting uncomfortably in the hard plastic seat and trying not to look nervous. I wore a full guide's kit complete with body armor, water bottle, utility belt, and survival gear. It was heavy, it was awkward, and I was not as familiar with the equipment as I should have been.

However, I quite liked the gun Charles had assigned me. It was a Mordecai Avenger .323 rifle, military-grade, with a fifty-round magazine and capable of both semi-automatic and fully automatic fire. Charles knew I could handle a gun, and his customary scowl had even evaporated momentarily when he saw my marksmanship scores. Thanks to my father and Uncle Morgan, I had grown up handling rifles, and I had taken to the Mordecai Avenger quite well. Granted, it was a bit more gun than I was used to, weighing about a kilo more than my trusty old Monster Hunter .224, but the basic principles were the same—stance, sighting, aiming, and then pull the trigger.

"Listen up, people!" shouted Charles over the roar of the quadcopter's engines. We all had an earpiece in our right ears and a microphone on our collars. It would have been easier to hear him with headphones, but walking around the jungles of Arborea with a pair of headphones was a stupendously bad idea and a great way to miss an audible warning that might save your life. "We are three klicks out from the target—one mature male tankstrider, no mate, and no attendant young. This is our designated kill for this hunt!"

"Ha!" said Rogson, his eyes glittering. "Time to shine, gentlemen! One shot, one kill!"

"Finance Director Rogson has chartered this expedition," said Charles, taking the long black tube of a rocket launcher from its rack on the wall. A rocket had already been loaded in the launcher, jutting from the business end like a diamond of gray metal. "Therefore Finance Director Rogson will fire the killing shot. Remember, the weak spot on a tankstrider's exoskeleton is directly behind the cranial fan, where the head joins with the thorax…"

"Yes, yes, I know all this," said Rogson. "I read the briefing packet."

Charles stared at him. Before the intensity of that disapproving gaze, the wealthy corporate executive swallowed, nodded, and gestured for him to continue. Or maybe it was just the sight of Arborea's wild jungles blurring past outside the window. The danger lurking in the leafy green depths had a way of putting one's mortality into perspective. All the money in the thousand words couldn't save you from an enraged stonesteer or the venom of a slabsnake… but it could hire the right men and equipment to deal with them.

"The pilot will line up the shot," said Charles. "If it goes amiss, we shall employ one of our contingency plans. Once the tankstrider is down, we shall land, collect trophies, harvest the meat, and… take pictures, I believe?"

"Very much so," said Rogson. "A group picture. I definitely want to be holding the rocket launcher in the picture. Think how it will look in the board room!"

"Yes," said Charles. "Pilot Hobson, our ETA?"

Hobson's voice crackled over my ear pieces. "Four minutes. I'm taking us down below the upper canopy."

"Stations, people!" said Charles.

I shifted in my seat, checking the Avenger one last time, and the pilot steered the quadcopter below the upper canopy of the jungle. The jungles of Arborea are just as immense as the animals, and some of the larger trees could easily reach fifteen hundred feet tall. From a distance, they looked like small green mountains. Consequently, there were multiple layers of canopies, with different winged predators lurking on each of the levels. Two of Charles's guides moved to the side doors of the quadcopter, rifles ready in their hands. Most of the winged predators would stay away from the noise the quadcopter generated, but some of them would not, and occasionally a really ambitious tromosaur clambered its way up a tree to attack its prey from above, and nothing except sonic alarms or a hail of bullets would drive them off.

Our descent was uneventful, and the quadcopter slipped through a gap in the massive branches to reach the lowest level of the jungle, just two hundred feet above the ground itself. It was gloomy down here, with occasional shafts of sunlight stabbing through the gaps in the canopy, and most of the vegetation let out a pale green glow. Frankly, it looked like a bizarre and badly misplaced city nightclub. The vegetation somehow produced its own light for photosynthesis or something. I had absolutely no idea how that worked, but then, I was a mechanic, not a biologist.

The tankstrider lumbered through the jungle a hundred meters in front of us.

The first time I saw a tankstrider, my first thought was that it was a building that had somehow grown legs and decided to go for a stroll through the jungles of Arborea. It was a huge creature, nearly a hundred meters long, with six thick legs and a fat tail that dragged along behind it through the foliage. The tankstrider kind of looked like a combination of an armadillo, an army ant, and a triceratops. Because of the vicious nature of Arborea's ecology, a tankstrider possessed both an internal skeleton and an exoskeleton of gleaming black and brown armor, armor that could shrug off anything short of ship-mounted railguns or missiles.

Which was why we were hunting it with a rocket launcher, not our Avengers.

Even with a rocket launcher, a tankstrider still had only one vulnerable point. Like an ancient triceratops, it had a massive bony frill rising from the back of its head that shielded its neck. Beneath the frill, where the head joined to the neck, was a vulnerable point full of nerve clusters and blood vessels, and a hit there could kill a tankstrider in short order. Of course, even without the exoskeleton, a tankstrider's hide was tough enough to shrug off most bullets. Something like a .50 caliber mini-gun or a plasma rifle would have been able to chew through the tankstrider's hide, but the noise or the heat would draw the gargantuan creature's attention and likely prove fatal long before the bullets or the plasma shells did any lasting damage.

So, a rocket launcher. A well-placed rocket was the only way, short of orbital bombardment, to take down a tankstrider. Of course, if the rocket missed the weak spot, it would only enrage the tankstrider, and if Hobson didn't get us out of reach quickly enough, the tankstrider would take the quadcopter down and smash it to bits with little difficulty. We had one shot to kill the tankstrider or the hunt would be a bust.

And we were trusting Lucius Rogson to make that shot.

Sweat trickled down my back as I watched him fumble with the rocket launcher, and not just from the constant oppressive humidity of Arborea. We were trusting in Rogson to make the shot, and Rogson was kind of an idiot. To be fair, he had paid an enormous sum of money for the privilege of killing a tankstrider, but I wouldn't have trusted Rogson to cut bread for me, let alone to shoot a rocket at a tankstrider.

Fortunately, Charles did everything he could to stack the deck. He told Rogson how to hold the rocket launcher, how to aim it, and in the process more or less aimed it for him. He shouted directions to Hobson, and the pilot got the quad-copter as low as he dared and as close as he dared without drawing the tankstrider's attention. The beast continued its leisurely stroll through the jungle, leaving a trail of crushed vegetation in its wake, though Arborea's insane ecology meant most of those plants would have regrown within a day or two.

"Steady," said Charles. "Steady… steady… fire!"

His voice cracked like a whip in my earpiece, and Rogson squeezed the trigger.

There was a whooshing noise, a roar, and the rocket erupted from the black tube on a plume of white smoke. I watched in frozen suspense as the rocket hurtled from the quadcopter's side door and covered the distance to the tankstrider. For an instant, I was utterly sure that Rogson had missed, and I only hoped the rocket would miss the tankstrider entirely and explode in the jungle without drawing the creature's attention.

Then the rocket slipped past the edge of the bony frill, vanishing against the back of the tankstrider's neck, and exploded with a flare of fire.

"Get us up!" shouted Charles. "Up! Up!"

The quadcopter rose, the engines howling.

"Did I hit it?" said Rogson. "Did I hit it?"

The tankstrider reared back with a roar of anger and pain, its legs lashing at the ground, its thick tail whipping back and forth, its massive armored beak snapping. I had a brief vision of that beak closing around the quadcopter and crushing it the way Tanner crushed walnut shells. The tankstrider let out another bellow, shuddered, and collapsed to the jungle floor with a thunderous crash.

The creature remained motionless, and the only sound in the quadcopter was the roar of the rotors.

"I did hit it!" said Rogson. "It's down! Is it dead?" He sounded as excited as a child who had hit a baseball for the first time, and with the sudden release of nervous tension, it was all I could do not to burst out laughing. All the same, it was an awesome sight.

"Congratulations, Finance Director Rogson," said Charles. "You have successfully claimed a tankstrider as a prize." The Bodyguard grinned and clapped his employer on the shoulder. "Pilot Hobson! Take us down to ground level. Guides, prepare for harvesting and guard protocol." Charles leveled a thick finger at me. "Indentured Worker Hammond, stay with me."

"What should I do?" I said.

"Watch for tromosaurs," said Charles, checking his own rifle one last time, "and if you see one, shoot it until it stops moving."

Hobson could have descended straight down to the jungle floor, but instead, he took a leisurely flyby, circling over the down tankstrider. The reason for that became apparent when the Lawyer leaned out the side door, holding an expensive camera. Rogson wanted footage of his conquest, no doubt to lord it over his hated rivals on the board. I suppose it was good advertising for Safari Company. Maybe in a few weeks, the rest of Rogson's board would show up with money in hand.

At last Hobson set the quadcopter down on the jungle floor, and we disembarked. Charles, the other guides, and I went first, looking back and forth for signs of predators. The tankstrider was a lot of meat, and that much meat would draw the attention of every scavenger for miles. Still, nothing stirred at the base of the massive trees, though the endless drone of insects filled my ears. The smell was perhaps the most overwhelming part of it all. The quadcopter had smelled of metal and gun oil and too many sweating men in too small of a space, but nothing smelled like the jungles of Arborea. It was a mixture of rotting vegetation and strange spores and odd fragrances from the flowers, overlaid by the ozone-like odor of the dead tankstrider.

Nothing on New Princeton had smelled like that, nothing at all, and I felt very, very far from home.

I stayed near Charles, and at his direction four of the guides spread out, watching the jungle for any sign of predators. Two of the guides went to assist Rogson and his minions. Rogson started by posing for photographs, the rocket launcher slung over his shoulder and one foot upon the tankstrider's side, beaming triumphantly. Meanwhile, a half-dozen tread-mounted drones rolled free of the helicopter. They would claim pieces of the tankstrider's side as trophies, as well as cutting chunks of meat for steaks. Tankstrider meat was edible, though I thought it tasted a little too bitter. In a few days, once all the meat had either been scarfed down by scavengers or eaten up by the jungle's insatiable blanket of bacteria, the Safari Company would send out an expedition to claim the exoskeleton and the bones. Tankstrider bone and chitin were tough, and had dozens of commercial applications.

I considered the dead tankstrider for a while. I know I should have felt sadness at the passing of such a giant creature and all that, or so the EcoMin broadcasts claimed in their lectures about the evils of hunting, but I didn't. The creature was just too big. And too alien.

"Pay attention," snapped Charles. "You can look at the pictures later."

I scowled, but he was right. I turned my attention back to the jungle as Rogson posed and the whirring drones went about their work.

So I saw the rippling distortion first.

At first, I thought my eyes were tricking me. It was hot out, really hot, and the ripples looked like the mirages over asphalt on a hot day. Except we were in the middle of the jungle, with no asphalt anywhere for miles, and the sun couldn't punch down this far to the jungle floor. So there were no reason for the air to ripple like that.

Except, of course, for the stealthing of a tromosaur.

"Charles," I said.

"I see it," said Charles. "Everyone, be aware we have a tromosaur sighting." The guides straightened up, Avengers rock-steady in their hands as they looked for targets. "Indentured Worker Hammond, it's closest to you. Take it down. Single shots, controlled spread."

I knew all that, and on the range I would have been irritated, but watching that air-ripple creep towards me was disturbing, and Charles's orders helped me stay focused.

I sighted down the weapon's length, took aim, and squeezed the trigger. I hit on my first shot, and the ripple expanded, rocking back.

The tromosaur shifted into the visible light spectrum a moment later.

It looked a lot like a dinosaur covered in mottled gray-and-green scales. I hadn't known what a dinosaur was until I came to Arborea, but Kayla had pointed me to an article on the topic. Apparently on ancient Earth, long before Man's diaspora across the Thousand Worlds, there had been a kind of big reptile called a dinosaur. Much later, after they had all gone extinct, humans discovered hyperspace and spread out across the Thousand Worlds, and an expedition found Arborea.

The tromosaurs ate them all, leaving no survivors.

After that, a second and better-armed expedition arrived to investigate the fate of the first one, and brought back word of tromosaurs. They looked a great deal like the kind of Terran dinosaur called a "velociraptor," albeit bigger, with thicker muscles and larger claws, and scales that could blend near-perfectly with their surroundings, and eyes like yellow crystals. The second expedition named the creatures "tromosaurs", which was an ancient Earth term for "nightmare lizard" or something like that.

Needless to say, the tromosaurs made the fangwolves back home look like newborn kittens.

The tromosaur staggered from the impact of my shot, its camouflage vanishing, and I felt the creature's attention turn towards me. It hurtled towards me, and I squeezed off three more rounds. The first two hit its chest, and the third went right through its skull. The tromosaur went into a weird dance, its thick tail jerking like a whip, and then collapsed to the jungle floor.

"Good shot," said Charles. "Let the official log reflect that Indentured Worker Hammond claimed one tromosaur kill." Had Hoskins been obliged to pay me, my next paycheck would have carried a nice bonus.

"Boss," said another of the guides, a hard-faced man named Warner. "Three more coming in, thirty degrees from the north."

"Two coming from the south," said another guide.

"The smell of the tankstrider's blood is drawing them," said Charles. "Warner, shoot the nearest one. See if that scares them off." Only two things repulsed tromosaurs. They hated sounds on certain sonic frequencies inaudible to humans, and the biologists thought it was because those frequencies mimicked the sounds tromosaurs made to warn each other of danger. The other thing was the scent of their own blood, which in sufficient quantities would drive off a tromosaur.

Sometimes.

Warner pivoted, raised his Avenger, and started shooting. He put four quick shots into the nearest tromosaur, two of them through its chest and the other two through its heart. The tromosaur rippled as it became visible once more, and the creature staggered and fell into a motionless heap, its tail coiling up in death. For the first time, I felt a little flicker of fear. The tankstriders were dangerous and alien but didn't care about humans... but the tromosaurs were both alien and dangerous and they really liked to eat human flesh.

And the remaining tromosaurs did not stop advancing towards us.

"They're not backing off," said Warner, retreating a few steps.

"I thought the smell of their own blood always scared them off," I said, trying to watch as many of the rippling distortions as I could. The fear was getting worse. Trying to watch a stealthed tromosaur gave me a headache, and I had the overwhelming feeling that one of the creatures was creeping up behind me.

"The smell of the dead tankstrider must be overwhelming the other scents," said Charles. "Finance Director Rogson! Defensive position."

"But..." started Rogson, lowering his rocket launcher as the two guides nearest to him turned their attention from the harvesting drones, their Avengers pointed out.

"Defensive position!" barked Charles in a voice that made Rogson jump and scurry for the quadcopter, the Bodyguard and the Lawyer trailing after him. "Pilot Hobson, prepare the quadcopter's weapons. Guides, activate your sonic alarms."

The sonic alarm was a black bracelet wound around my left wrist. I tapped it, and a blue LED flicked on, the bracelet vibrating. I couldn't hear the sound it made, but the tromosaurs did, and the rippling blurs stopped as the other guides activated their alarms. My fear eased a little. If the sound frightened off the tromosaurs...

The bracelet on Warner's wrist gave off a high-pitched screech.

The tromosaurs went motionless, shifting back into the visible spectrum, and every one of them looked at Warner with their bright, glittering eyes. The sonic alarm was supposed to ward off the tromosaurs, but Warner's was malfunctioning. The sound was exactly like the hunting cry of a tromosaur. In fact, unless I missed my guess, it was the cry they used when summoning others to the hunt.

The sound was coming with ear-splitting volume from Warner's wrist.

"Turn it off!" shouted Charles. "Turn it off!"

"I'm trying!" said Warner, clawing at his wrist. He lowered the Avenger, trying to get the bracelet off. "It's not—"

The remaining tromosaurs charged at him. I opened fire, and I got two of them, but three tromosaurs plowed into Warner, knocking him to the ground. At once they started biting and ripping at him, hammering the massive claws on their feet into his torso. He wore body armor like we all did, but it couldn't hold up for long against that kind of abuse.

I sprinted towards Warner to give myself a better shot, stopped and fired, and managed to get the three tromosaurs off him. Warner scrambled backward, panting, and I saw blood on his armor from where the tromosaurs' fangs and claws had gotten through. A dozen more of the creatures stalked towards us, eyes fixed upon Warner.

"Hammond!" said Charles. "Break it! Break the alarm!"

"Sorry about this, man," I said. I raised my boot and brought it down hard onto Warner's left arm. Warner screamed in pain, and I heard the crack as I broke his wrist, but the sonic alarm shattered too. The high-pitched screech abruptly vanished.

The remaining tromosaurs froze again. Likely they could hear the other bracelets once more. Charles and the other guides opened up, and this time the tromosaurs had had enough. They turned and fled back into the jungle, vanishing into the trees.

The last tromosaur fled, and I lowered my Avenger, breathing hard, my ears still ringing.

"You actually impressed Charles," said Tanner two days later as I had dinner with him and Kayla. "That never happens."

"I read the report," said Kayla. "If you hadn't acted so quickly, Warner would be dead."

"Yeah," I said. "I just wish I hadn't smashed Warner's bracelet. I wanted to have a closer look at it."

Kayla shrugged. "It must have malfunctioned."

"Or maybe it was sabotaged," said Tanner. "A sonic alarm shouldn't even be able to make a noise like that. Makes you wonder what else might have been sabotaged. We've had so many inexplicable problems with equipment failures and malfunctions."

"You know what EcoMin is like, Winston," said Kayla. "They'll do whatever they think they can get away with." There was sudden heat in her voice. I wondered what the ministry had done to her family, but there was no way I was dumb enough to ask her in front of Tanner. "If a faction in there wants Safari Company to fail, they'll do whatever they can to make it fail."

"Well, then," said Tanner, "we'll just have to make sure they fail."

We did. The next year went on more or less as I've described. I became sort of the jack-of-all-trades of Outpost Town, fixing robot and mechanical failures and going out on expeditions with Charles and the other guides. Charles decided that he approved of me, and every few weeks would bring me on a hunting expedition when he was short-handed. During that year, I found a dozen different major equipment malfunctions that would have killed people, but thankfully Tanner and I managed to repair them first. We did have losses, but mostly when people were stupid and wandered outside the sonic fence and the tromosaurs got them.

It seemed obvious that an EcoMin faction did indeed want to shut down the Safari Company by any means possible.

It was a logical conclusion… and it was also completely wrong.

We were about to find that out the hard way.

Chapter 3
Spit and Polish

I spent the day repairing some harvest drones, and went to the Tanners' apartment for dinner, where I heard the news.

"Mr. Royale's coming here?" I said.

"In person," said Kayla, setting out a dish of tromosaur fajitas. Given how many tromosaurs we had to shoot, it was a good thing they were edible, though I always thought they tasted a little off. Fortunately, enough spice covered that up.

"And," said Tanner, scowling at the phone in his hand, "a lot of other important people. Seems like the board has decided to go all out for the grand opening. Just what we need."

The last six weeks had been busy, with nonstop work. The board of Safari Company had decided that Outpost Town was ready for a grand opening. Clients had visited Arborea on a regular basis for the last year, but everything was still in trial mode—a beta test, I think they called it in software development. Despite endless glitches and sabotage attempts, we hadn't lost any important clients, and the board was ready to open Outpost Town for business.

And in another six months, my indenture would be up, and I could do whatever I wanted.

It was an odd thought… but I think I wanted to stay on with Safari Company. I liked the work, both the mechanical stuff and the expeditions, and if I hadn't been indentured, I would have made a lot of money from expeditions. Hoskins had invited me to stay on after my indenture was up, and so had Charles.

And it wasn't boring. Wilson City had been boring.

I wondered what Mr. Royale would think, and I was looking forward to asking him.

"It'll be good publicity for the Company," said Kayla, ever the optimist.

"If it was just Ian, I wouldn't mind," said Tanner. "But the entire board is coming to inspect Outpost Town for the grand opening. Worse, a small army of EcoMin officials are coming for the festivities."

"Ugh," I said. I hadn't thought about Theresa in months, but I wasn't thrilled at the prospect of meeting her mother again.

"Including, if the rumors are true," said Tanner, "Minister Paul Valier himself."

Kayla almost dropped her spoon. "What?"

"Evidently, the reason Safari Company hasn't been shut down is that Valier himself thinks it's a good idea," said Tanner. "More likely, he just needs the money. The Acadarchy isn't swimming in cash at the moment... Kayla?"

I blinked. Kayla was almost always collected and calm and even cheerful, but now her lips were pressed tight together, spots of color flaring in her cheeks, tears starting in her eyes. But it wasn't because she was sad. She looked like she was about to start crying in sheer rage.

"Sorry," said Kayla, waving her hand in an indistinct gesture. "Sorry. That just... upset me more than I thought.

That scoundrel wrecked my father's farm, and to hear that he's coming to Arborea… sorry."

"Hey," said Tanner, scooting his chair towards her and putting his arm around her shoulders. She leaned against him, still shivering a little.

"Um," I said. "Right. Uh… I should go. Thanks for dinner."

"There's no reason you shouldn't know," said Kayla. "Did you ever wonder why Winston and I don't have children?"

I had.

"Of course not," I said.

"My dad was a farmer on New Princeton," said Kayla. "When Paul Valier was rising up through the Ministry ranks, he was in charge of pesticide testing. Well, he had a spiffy new pesticide, and he insisted that my father replace his old pesticides and use this stuff instead. Promised it would increase crop yields by two hundred percent, but like everything else the Ministry says, it's a lie. The stuff killed all our crops and caused my mother to die of cancer. Valier blamed my father for it, said he mishandled the pesticide and sued him into bankruptcy. There was one other little side effect I found out later… I can't carry a baby past three or four months without miscarrying. None of my sisters can."

"Oh," I said. "I'm sorry."

"We lost everything," said Kayla, "and now that horrible man is the Ecology Minister."

We sat in silence for a moment.

"If it makes you feel better," I said, "I got arrested for spray-painting graffiti onto Valier's official portrait on the ministry's campus."

Kayla let out a hiccupping little laugh. "I knew there was a reason I liked you, Sam."

Still, as much as Kayla detested the ministry in general, and Valier in particular, I wondered if that was a good sign. Valier wouldn't be making the trip out to Arborea if he didn't approve of the Safari Company, and as long as Valier approved of the Safari Company, a thousand minor lapses wouldn't be enough to shut us down. All we had to do was to keep Valier from getting eaten by a tromosaur, and Safari Company could have its grand opening and start pulling in more clients. Even better, once the Company was a done deal, maybe the faction in the Ministry that opposed us would move on to easier targets.

I doubted it would be that easy. Plus, a little paranoid voice in my head wondered if the anti-Safari Company faction in the ministry would use Valier's visit as an opportunity to assassinate him and install someone more pliable as minister. Some of the sabotage attempts we had seen, like Warner's malfunctioning sonic alarm, could have gotten someone killed. Tanner agreed that it was a possibility, and urged me to keep my eyes open.

Tanner tended to agree with that little paranoid voice in my head most of the time.

Everyone at Outpost Town starting pulling double-shifts to prepare for the visit of the board and the Minister. If I hadn't been indentured, I would have made a killing on overtime. Apparently, Valier was bringing his entire entourage of body-guards and assistants and lackeys, and he had also invited along a bunch of illustrious guests. I suppose that was good. If the grand opening went well, the Safari Company might have a bunch of new clients, and since I wanted to hire on with the Company once my indenture was over, the growing number of clients was a good sign.

After three months of nonstop work, we were as ready as we could manage for the day of the big visit.

I had spent the last two weeks checking over every service drone, hospitality robot, and harvesting drone in Outpost Town. Tanner suspected that someone might have reprogrammed a drone to kill a guest, and after some of the sabotage attempts we had seen, it was a reasonable fear. Fortunately, I didn't find anything wrong, other than the usual breakdowns caused by wear and tear. In fact, in the last six weeks before the visit, it seemed like everything had gone smooth as butter on hot glass. No sabotaged parts and equipment came in the supply shipments, none of the cleaning drones went berserk and tried to wash the guests, and the sonic fence didn't malfunction. Maybe that meant the anti-Company faction within the ministry had decided to cut its losses.

But I couldn't make myself believe that. I had been a farmer for too long. Uncle Morgan had been fond of saying that whenever it looked things were going smoothly, that was the time to anticipate trouble.

So I waited with Tanner and Kayla on the landing pad, watching as the ships descended from the cloudy sky. I hadn't been sure what to wear, so I had finally gone with the body armor and jumpsuit guides wore on hunting expeditions, mostly because it looked impressive. Tanner wore his Security Director's uniform. Kayla cleaned up nicely in a dress and high heels, and I was trying hard not to stare too hard at her. All the women at Outpost Town were married, so there hadn't been any opportunities for me to meet girls anyway. Usually, workers rotated back to New Princeton for some leave every three months, but I was indentured, so I had been here for a year.

Finding a girlfriend was something I could think about after we had survived the grand opening. It wasn't as if I'd had any time for one anyway.

"There's Royale's ship," said Tanner, pointing towards a boxy light freighter settling down on the far end of the landing field.

"Let's go say hello," said Kayla.

We crossed the field as more ships touched down, the humid air heavy with the harsh smell of ozone from the ships antigrav units. The ships disgorged bodyguards and dignitaries, all of them heading towards Outpost Town's big banquet hall. The guests would have a meal there, Hoskins and the board would give speeches, and Charles and the guides would take some of the more influential guests out on hunts. I figured I would wind up accompanying Charles on one of the hunts unless the kitchen drones suffered a mass breakdown.

Mr. Royale's freighter lowered its boarding ramp, and to my surprise, several men in the severe black uniforms of New Princeton's Security Ministry descended to the landing field. Was Mr. Royale in trouble? Tanner and Kayla stopped a few yards away. Tanner didn't look alarmed, so I relaxed, but only a little.

A moment later Mr. Royale descended the ramp, wearing his usual white suit, accompanied by a battered-looking man in the uniform of a Security Ministry colonel. The left side of the colonel's mouth turned in a sour-looking frown, left by the vicious-looking scar along his cheek. The wound must have been too severe for reconstructive surgery to repair. His ears looked like cauliflower, and his nose had been broken and reset several times.

"Well, well," said Mr. Royale, shaking Tanner's hand. "Winston Tanner, Kayla Tanner, and Sam Hammond. It's good to see all three of you."

"Good to see you, sir," I said, shaking Mr. Royale's hand.

"Winston here has been telling me good things about you," said Mr. Royale.

"I have?" said Tanner. "That doesn't sound like me, Spraycan. When would I do a thing like that?"

Kayla gave him a gentle elbow to the ribs. "I'm glad to see you again, Ian. It's hard to find civilized conversation out here on the frontier."

"Well," said Mr. Royale. "It's hard to find civilized conversation on New Princeton as well." He gestured to the battered colonel. "This is Colonel Cassius Argent of the Security Ministry. The Security Ministry has expressed an interest in renting our little outpost here as a training facility for elite troops, and the good colonel has been assigned to view our operations firsthand."

Argent nodded. "Mr. Royale was kind enough to offer the use of his ship for transit here." His voice was a little slurred, and he had to pronounce his words carefully, probably from the damage to his lips and jaws. "Unlike those perfumed princelings at EcoMin, we in the Security Ministry do not have unlimited expense accounts, and we must guard our finances accordingly." He beckoned, and four hard-looking men in black uniforms stepped to his sign. "Mr. Royale, good day. Thank you again for the lift."

Argent strode off, his four men following him.

"You're not in trouble, are you?" said Tanner at last.

"No," said Mr. Royale. "Well, no more than usual. As far as I can tell, Colonel Argent merely wanted a ride to Arborea, and he wanted to do it off the books. He and his soldiers were pleasant enough company, if not terribly inclined towards small talk. I suspect he is investigating one of the potential guests, and wished to find a way to Outpost Town that was, shall we say, below the radar of the other ministries."

"I hope he doesn't arrest whoever he's after here," I said. "That might be bad for the Company."

"Not necessarily," said Mr. Royale. "It could be good PR. Show how we are cooperating with the law and all that. Given all the harassment the Ecology Ministry has given us, we don't want to be seen as shifty. Paul Valier might have come around to supporting the Company, but he won't be Minister forever, and some crusading young firebrand might take his place. Best to have as many friends as possible if that happens." He grinned at us. "Though thanks to your efforts, that will be easier to arrange. Hoskins wrote quite highly of all the sabotage attempts you thwarted. Sam, you did so well it almost makes me wish we were paying you."

"Almost?" I said.

"Well, not quite that much," said Mr. Royale. "But if you want a job with the Safari Company when your indenture is over, whether as a guide or in the mechanical services department or even both, it's yours."

That was good to hear. Hoskins had promised me a job, but Hoskins could be replaced and fired if the board wanted, and I had never known Mr. Royale to go back on his word.

"The board has a meeting before the dinner," said Mr. Royale, "but you're all my guests at the dinner, of course. I expect Minister Valier will want to give a speech…"

"Let's hope there is a lot of alcohol," said Kayla.

Mr. Royale smiled. "I'm sure the Minister's wit is matched only by his brevity. Once his oration finally wraps up, tomorrow the guides will be taking the board members and the prominent guests on tours of the neighboring jungle, a sightseeing tour of sorts. Perhaps we'll see a tankstrider or a platewhale."

"Might be another revenue stream in that," said Tanner. "Not everyone's cut out to go hunting alien game with a rocket launcher, and not everyone can afford it, either."

"That," said Mr. Royale, "is an excellent thought. We were looking at putting together some kind of group tour package… ah, we'd best wait a moment and let them pass."

A group of men strode down the landing pad. Six of them wore dark suits with sunglasses and earpieces and had the look of expensive private security experts. Tanner's lip curled in an instinctive sneer. He had expounded to me, more than once, about his low opinion of the kind of private security that went around dressed in expensive suits. In their midst marched a heavyset man wearing a suit that probably cost more than all the bodyguards' clothes put together, scowling at a phone he held in his left hand while a beleaguered-looking woman with the air of an executive assistance towed three suitcases behind her. The heavyset man did not look up as he passed, but several of the bodyguards scowled in our direction.

"Friend of yours, sir?" I said.

"No," said Mr. Royale.

"That," said Tanner, "is Alexander Toulon, chairman and chief executive officer of the Toulon Group."

"Oh," I said, trying to think of where I had heard the name before. "That's a big… chemical company, isn't? From New

Princeton, based in Roosevelt City?" I was sure I had heard the name before. I looked over at Tanner and saw that he was holding Kayla's hand, that her lips were pressed into a thin, hard line as she stared at Toulon.

Oh, yeah. That new pesticide that Valier had pushed upon Kayla's family? Toulon Group had manufactured it.

"Ian," said Kayla in a soft voice.

"Yes?" said Mr. Royale.

"Are all our customers going to be scum like him?" said Kayla.

"A fair percentage," said Mr. Royale without rancor. "I'm afraid a man doesn't get to Toulon's level of wealth and power without leaving a large amount of harm in his wake. I hope overcharging Toulon a ridiculous amount for... well, absolutely everything in Outpost Town, is a sufficient revenge for the time being."

Kayla didn't say anything, but she did smile, although I thought it was a little forced. I hoped Tanner had the good sense to keep her away from Toulon. Having a CEO for an interplanetary corporation poisoned or stabbed to death during the grand opening would not be good for the Company. On the other hand, if the tromosaurs got him...

I put that line of thought out of my head, and then forgot it a second later when I saw the Ecology Minister, Paul Valier himself.

An Acadarchy shuttle had put down at the edge of the landing field, closest to Outpost Town's most expensive hotel, and it disgorged a troop of EcoMin's black-uniformed Special Operations soldiers, which made sense of Colonel Argent's decision to hitch a ride with Mr. Royale. A moment later, Paul Valier came down the ramp, wearing an expensive gray suit. He looked exactly the way he had in the portrait I had defaced, tall and lean, with thick black hair greying at the temples and a close-cropped black beard. He looked just like you'd want a politician to look, strong and commanding and trustworthy, and I could easily imagine him giving a speech to keep the population calm during a crisis.

Of course, it was all a lie. I wondered if there was such a thing as an honest politician. I suppose anything was possible, but I had yet to meet one.

"Right," said Tanner. "We've got work to do. I've got to keep order. All these bodyguards with entitled bosses add up to a lot of twitchy trigger fingers. Spraycan, stay by the kitchens. Hoskins wants you to fix any of the kitchen and serving drones if they break down."

"Spraycan?" said Mr. Royale, raising his eyebrows.

I sighed. "Don't ask."

For once, something went right. The grand banquet welcoming the board and the various VIP guests went off with only minor hitches. Only three of the kitchen drones and two of the serving drones malfunctioned, and I managed to get them working again in short order. The kitchens outdid themselves preparing a feast of tankstrider steaks and fruits and vegetables harvested from the jungle. I filled a plate for myself and sat in a folding chair by the kitchen doors and listened as Hoskins welcomed the guests, followed by a round of speeches from the more important VIPs. Valier's speech went on the longest, praising the Safari Company as an exciting new way for mankind to interact with the environment of an alien world while respecting its ecology and still maintaining a profit. It would have been a rousing speech, if not for the dozens of

EMSO soldiers that patrolled the hall while he spoke. Uncle Morgan had always complained about the Ministry's soldiers during his rants, and Kayla had spoken harshly about them a few times.

I guess those Special Operations included protecting the Ecology Minister from assassination, because according to the guest list, Valier had brought a hundred of them with him. I made sure to stay well away from them. They stared at everything with flat, unfriendly eyes, and carried a lot of heavy weaponry.

Yet despite all the guns and twitchy fingers in the room, the banquet went off without a hitch. People even seemed to have a good time. I bet the liquor helped with that.

The next morning, we prepared to take the guests not suffering hangovers up in the quadcopters for tours of the nearby jungle. Every guide was taking a flight, and so Charles recruited me to help, along with all of Tanner's security personnel. I wound up on Hobson's quadcopter again, with me, Tanner, and Charles escorting Mr. Royale as he received a tour of the local jungles. That reminded me of my first flight on Hobson's quadcopter, and my encounter with the tromosaurs that had nearly killed Warner. I was a little worried, although I knew nothing ought to go wrong since we weren't even hunting anything, just giving Mr. Royale a tour of the local jungle. Yet after a year of dealing with malfunctions and glitches, both deliberate and accidental, I had gotten a lot more cautious. So I checked and double-checked my body armor and my Avenger, loaded up on ammunition and supplies, and helped Charles and Hobson double-check the supplies in the quadcopter. I also checked everyone's sonar alarms, just to be sure. But all of them worked normally.

Maybe some of Tanner's paranoia was wearing off on me.

"Board Member Royale," said Charles as we finished loading the quadcopter for its flight. "Welcome! I am Senior Guide Hiram Charles, and I shall be overseeing this flight."

"Senior Guide Charles," said Mr. Royale, shaking his hand. "I'm glad to meet you. Hoskins and the others have had many good things to say about your work."

"Thank you, Board Member," said Charles. "And yet, excellence must be applied in all matters regardless of praise or criticism."

Mr. Royale blinked, then smiled faintly and made a formal little bow to Charles. "A commendable attitude, Senior Guide."

I tried not to laugh. I figured he had Charles's number already.

"Let us begin the safety briefing now," said Charles, and he launched into his usual speech, pointing out the emergency exits from the quadcopter and the crash features and detailing how to use a sonic alarm properly. Most of the guests looked bored at this point, but Mr. Royale paid close attention. He was too polite to do otherwise... and maybe after his encounter with the fangwolves at Uncle Morgan's farm back on New Princeton, he knew to pay attention to these kind of warnings.

Once Charles had finished, we loaded into the quadcopter. Hobson started the engines, and we took off, leaving Outpost Town behind and soaring over the jungle. It was, at least by the standards of Arborea, a beautiful day. We flew forty yards over the highest canopy, the sky overhead mostly overcast, but huge rents in the clouds sent shafts of blazing sunlight down into the jungle, and where the light touched the tops of the trees, they turned a shade of green so brilliant it almost looked unreal.

"If you will look to your left, Board Member Royale," said Charles, "you will see the most common species of tree found on this continent of Arborea." It was a little strange to see him acting like a lowly tour guide, but he was Senior Guide, and Charles took that responsibility as seriously as he took everything else. "We have located a pod of platewhales, and will go on a flyby. Platewhales are primarily vegetarian, though in times of scarcity they have been observed to expand their dietary spectrum."

A beep came over my earpiece.

"Charles, Tanner," said Hobson. "Something's up."

"What is it?" said Tanner.

"There's another quadcopter coming up right behind us," said Hobson.

"One of the other tours?" said Mr. Royale.

Tanner frowned. "None of the other tours should be coming this way. At least, they're not supposed to be. Get them on the radio, Hobson. See if they're having navigational trouble."

"Checking," said Hobson. "No, nothing. They're not answering."

I got up from my seat along the quadcopter's hull and made my way to the back hatch, peering through the two narrow viewports, the deck vibrating beneath my boots.

"Wait," I said. "Tanner, that's not one of our quadcopters."

"Are you sure?" said Tanner.

"Positive," I said. "I've been up in every single one of our quadcopters. That's not one of ours."

Tanner scowled. "One of our guests must have brought one of their own for a little unauthorized joyriding. Well, we'll charge them through the nose for that."

"Pilot Hobson," said Charles. "What kind of quadcopter is it? Do you recognize it?"

"Hang on," said Hobson. "It's a New Princeton Avionics AA-39 model, law enforcement configuration…"

"Law enforcement?" I said. That model sounded familiar, for some reason.

"EcoMin," said Mr. Royale. "Aside from the police, they are the only ministry that flies that particular model of quad. Their Special Operations squads use them."

I shared a look with Tanner. So why was a Special Operations quadcopter, which wasn't supposed to be on Arborea in the first place, following us while maintaining radio silence?

I could think of a couple different reasons, but all of them were bad.

"Hobson, raise Outpost Town," said Tanner. "Ask them what's going on."

There was silence on the earpiece again. I peered out the back viewports, watching the distant black speck of the following quadcopter. It didn't seem to be drawing any closer, but it was following us.

"Nothing," said Hobson. "Just static."

"I recommend an immediate return, Security Director Tanner," said Charles.

"Right," said Tanner. "You heard the man, Hobson. Get us back to town. Now."

"Acknowledged," said Hobson. He started to swing the craft around, and I grabbed at one of the ceiling straps to keep my balance.

And as he did, I saw the distant glare of orange-yellow light through the viewport. We hadn't gone all that far from Outpost Town yet, and if not for the trees it would have been visible. That meant sometimes I could see the lights from the buildings, but right now I only saw that harsh yellow-orange light from the direction of the settlement.

Like a really big fire.

"Tanner," I said. "Look at that. I think Outpost is on fire."

"What?" said Tanner.

"He's right," said Hobson, his voice grim. "I can see it from up here. We…"

A shrill alarm cut off his voice.

"Proximity alarm!" said Charles. "Assume crash positions!"

"Crash positions?" said Mr. Royale.

"That quad just fired a missile at us!" shouted Hobson. "I'm going evasive. Strap in!"

I scrambled into my seat along the wall, strapping myself in as the others hastened to follow suit. Even before I had the last strap buckled, Hobson threw the quadcopter down and to the left, my stomach jumping up to land somewhere next to my ears. The shrill alarm got louder, and as the quadcopter zigged and zagged, I saw a flare of fire through the rear viewports.

Hobson snarled. "Incoming! Hang on!

The quadcopter rolled as he jerked it to the right, and then… I don't remember the next few minutes clearly.

There was a tremendous roar, accompanied by the shriek of tearing metal and the howl of flames. For a moment I thought that I was spinning, and then I realized the quadcopter was spinning, which I supposed meant that I was spinning with it.

The quadcopter was going down. Or, to put it more bluntly, crashing.

There was a horrible shriek of ripping metal and an overwhelming crunching sound, and I felt as if I had been smashed by a giant fist that slammed into my entire body.

Then everything went black.

Chapter 4

The Most Dangerous Game

I don't think I was out for long.

The incessant beeping of some alarm or another woke me up.

I smelled smoke, and flickering yellow-orange light played across the walls. The electric lights had gone out, save for one that kept sputtering. Yellow-orange light… nothing in the quadcopter had that kind of glow. It looked a lot like a candle, come to think of it.

I smelled smoke too. Was something on fire?

That woke me up fast. Quadcopters had all sorts of flammable things in the engines, and if the fire got to the fuel cells, we were in a lot of trouble.

The memory of the missile and our crash came rushing back.

We were in a lot of trouble already.

I was still strapped into my seat along the wall, but I was lying on my back. That meant the quadcopter had landed on its side. My head felt fuzzy, but I didn't think I had a concussion. I'd had a few concussions when I had been younger, thanks to tractor drone-related accidents, and those felt different. No, I just felt bruised and sore.

But what about the others?

I turned my head, alarmed, and then felt a hand close around my left shoulder.

"Oh, good, you're awake," said Tanner. Sweat glittered on his broad face, and he was bleeding from a cut on his jaw and his temple, but he looked otherwise unhurt. "The others were conscious, so I got them out first. Thought I was going to have to cut you out of your restraints and carry you out."

"The others?" I said, fumbling with the release on my straps. "Are they…"

Tanner grimaced. "Hobson didn't make it. Branch went through the canopy and took his head off. A messy way to go." He shook his head. "Me, Charles, and Ian had a few scratches, but nothing serious. Can you walk?"

"Yeah," I said, pushing away the restraints and standing up. I was standing on the wall, which was the oddest feeling. "What are we going to do now?"

"We're heading back to Outpost Town," said Tanner, his voice decisive. "I think were only about fifteen kilometers away. We can do it on foot." He looked around the wrecked quadcopter. "Not that we have a choice."

"Fifteen kilometers of the Arborean jungle is… a lot," I said, calculating the odds in my head. They weren't good.

"Like I said, we don't have a choice," said Tanner. "There's something going on at Outpost Town. We're going to go back, find out what's happening, and shut it down."

I frowned. Paul Valier was there, and an EcoMin quadcopter had shot us down. That implied that someone in the Ecology Ministry had ordered our deaths, and probably that they had caused the fire or the explosion or whatever we had seen in the distance. Maybe Valier had been planning to kill us all the entire time. Except he couldn't do that, could he? I mean, the Acadarchy was corrupt, but they didn't go around shooting people and blowing stuff up as far as I'd ever heard. When they wanted to ruin someone, they used lawsuits and fines and armies of bureaucrats, not actual soldiers with actual guns.

But we were a long, long way from New Princeton, and maybe Valier thought he could get away with more on an alien planet.

"Come on," said Tanner. "Get your pack, get your Avenger, get your sonic alarm, and let's go."

I was already wearing my sonic alarm on my left wrist. My pack had ended up on the far side of the cabin, but fortunately, my rifle was still locked in the gun rack. Once I had retrieved my pack and the Avenger, I followed Tanner out the shattered side door and into the jungles of Arborea.

The musty, alien smell of the jungle filled my nostrils, along with the odor of burning fuel and smoke. There was also the smell of human blood. I caught a glimpse of poor Hobson in the cockpit as we passed the quadcopter's broken canopy, and I really wished that I hadn't looked. At least his death had been almost instantaneous.

Charles and Mr. Royale waited nearby, both carrying rifles. Charles scanned the jungle constantly, his eyes sliding back and forth with smooth, practiced motions. Mr. Royale merely looked tense, though he held his Avenger competently enough. I wondered where he had learned to shoot. I was grateful that Charles had persuaded him to wear body armor instead of his customary white suit.

"Pilot Hobson?" said Charles.

Tanner shook his head.

"Should we take his body back?" said Mr. Royale.

"We can't," said Tanner. "The smell will draw every scavenger in the jungle soon enough, not just the tromosaurs. If we carry him with us, we won't make it a kilometer."

"We should go now," said Charles. "If we move at once, the tromosaurs will likely be drawn to the smell of Hobson's blood."

"That's harsh," said Mr. Royale.

"It is, but it's necessary," said Tanner. "The jungle of Arborea does not forgive its mistakes."

"Nor do the men who shot us down," said Mr. Royale. "We had best move before the come to check on us."

Yeah. In the chaos of the crash I had all but forgotten about that.

"Wonder why they haven't come down and strafed us," said Tanner, looking up at the gloomy canopy. "Just to be sure."

Charles shook his head. "It takes time to safely navigate between the various layers of the canopy. They don't want to crash alongside us."

"But why didn't they kill us?" said Mr. Royale.

Tanner snorted. "They just did their best to do it."

"No," said Mr. Royale. "That missile could have wiped us out. Yet it was targeted at only one of our rotors. Look."

I wasn't an expert in demolitions, but I followed his pointing finger and saw that he was right. The quadcopter's aft starboard rotor had been reduced to twisted metal and melted plastic. I realized that it had been a disabling shot, designed to force us down. With only three rotors left, poor Hobson had still been able to force a crash landing, even if it had gotten him killed in the process. The missile could just have easily hit the passenger cabin, killing us all, or the fuel cells, blasting the quadcopter to molten shreds.

"So why make us crash?" said Tanner. "Why not just kill us? They're playing a dangerous game if they leave witnesses alive."

Mr. Royale gave him a sharp look. "What did you say?"

"I said it's stupid of them to leave witnesses alive," said Tanner.

"Dangerous," I said. "You said it was a dangerous game."

"So?" said Tanner with a scowl. "We have more important things to think about."

"Like getting away from here," said Charles.

"Yes," said Mr. Royale, though he still looked distracted. "I saw Valier reading something by that name on his tablet last night during the banquet."

I heard the drone of quadcopter rotors coming from overhead.

"Right," said Tanner. "We need to go. Charles, get..."

"Wait!" said Mr. Royale, a look of grim realization coming over his face. "Do we have any gas masks?"

"Gas masks?" said Tanner.

"They are attached to our packs, Board Member Royale," said Charles, reaching back and pulling out his own mask.

"Put them on," said Mr. Royale, fumbling for his own mask. "Do it! They're not going to shoot us. They're going to gas us first. Then they'll shoot us."

"Are you sure?" said Tanner.

"Entirely," said Mr. Royale, putting on his mask. "I think we've been conned, all of us. I'll explain if we live through the next five minutes." I pulled on my own gas mask, following the example of the older men. It wasn't a comfortable thing. The straps pulled at the back of my head, the edges dug into my face, and the goggles restricted by field of view.

"So you think they'll gas us and then come down to kill us?" said Tanner, incredulous.

"Almost certainly," said Mr. Royale. "But we're going to disrupt their plans."

"We should return to the quadcopter," said Charles. "We can lie in wait for them and ambush them there."

"I like the way you think, Senior Guide Charles," said Mr. Royale.

"Then move," said Tanner. "Ian, you and Spraycan go first. Charles and I will watch the doors. Go."

We scrambled into the wreckage of the quadcopter, climbing over the torn door and into the passenger cabin. Charles and Tanner positioned themselves by the door, rifles ready. I peered out one of the viewports, my heart racing, my mind spinning. I could not figure out why the Ministry quadcopter would gas us. I mean, obviously, they would gas us so it would be easier to kill us or take us prisoner, but this seemed like a really inefficient way to go about killing people. If they had wanted to kill us, it would have been easier to shoot the quadcopter out of the sky. If they wanted to take us prisoner, it would have made more sense to arrest us before we left Outpost Town in a quadcopter.

So just what were they doing?

I started to ask Mr. Royale about that book of his, and then I heard the whine of motors overhead.

The quadcopter that shot us down glided overhead, circling over the wreck. Up close, I saw that it was a lot smaller than our wrecked craft. The Safari Company's quadcopters had been designed to carry passengers, drones, and trophies from hunting kills. This quadcopter looked leaner and sleeker, with stubby wings holding weapons. It looked like a fighter, though it was big enough to hold maybe a dozen Ecology Ministry special operations troops.

The quadcopter circled over us twice more, scanning the wreckage, and then lifted up. A handful of small, shiny shapes fell from its belly and landed with dull clanks on the ground. They were canisters, and bright green warning labels covered their sides. I just had time to note the labels, and then a hissing sound filled my ears, the air over the canisters rippling.

I don't know how he knew, but Mr. Royale had been right. They were trying to gas us.

The quadcopter rose up as the canisters kept leaking gas and soon was out of sight once more.

"Should we go?" I whispered.

"No," said Tanner. "They'll be watching. If they see us with masks, they'll open fire or drop a bomb on our heads." A hard edge entered his voice. "Let the idiots land, and let them think they're taking helpless victims. We'll have a surprise for them."

"Sound tactical thinking, Security Director Tanner," said Charles.

"I'm glad you approve," said Tanner.

We waited ten minutes, and nothing happened. Then the quadcopter flew overhead once more, and dropped low, no more than a dozen yards overhead, the roar of the rotors filling my ears. They were blowing away the gas, which meant they were getting ready to land.

The quadcopter hovered for maybe another five minutes, and then it rotated and slowly descended to the ground, the engines shutting off with a whine.

"Get ready," breathed Tanner. "Don't do anything until I say the word."

I nodded and gripped my Avenger, checking it over one last time. The gun could switch between semi-automatic, burst mode, and full-automatic with a flick of a switch, though it wasn't terribly accurate on full-auto and would empty out its ammo supply in about two seconds. I flicked the switch to semi-automatic, made sure the safety was off, and waited.

The door on the quadcopter opened, and I braced myself for a dozen Ecology Ministry Special Operations goons in body armor to rush out, carrying military-grade combination gun/laser rifles.

I did not expect to see a short, fat man in an expensive suit stroll out, smoking a cigar with one hand and holding a pistol incompetently in his other. After him came three larger men, both in suits, two of them carrying pistols. The third man carried a rocket launcher, swinging it back and forth as if he feared that tromosaurs would erupt from the jungle at any moment.

I stared at them in surprise for a moment, and then my brain caught up to my eyes.

That was Alexander Toulon, chairman of the Toulon Group, strolling through the jungle with a pistol and a cigar with his bodyguards.

For some reason, a multi-billionaire CEO had just shot us down.

Tanner reached up and tapped the side of his head, turning on his earpiece's camera.

Toulon stopped a dozen yards from the wrecked helicopter, frowning. He lifted the cigar to his lips and took a long draw from it, blowing out a cloud of smoke. He was red-faced enough that it made him look like a tomato with a nicotine habit.

Then his red face spread into a delighted smile.

"That," he said, "was awesome. It really was. I mean, I had doubts when Valier pitched it to us… but, man! Did you see that quadcopter go down?"

"Yes, sir," said one of the bodyguards. "I was piloting."

"Worth every credit," said Toulon. "It's the thrill of the hunt. The essence of precivilization, you know." He took another draw on his cigar. "Also, the trophies." He raised his pistol. "I'll take the kill shots with this. I want to get pictures. You know, poses, that kind of thing."

"Do you want to shoot them in the quadcopter, sir?" said the bodyguard with the rocket launcher. "Or shall we bring them out?"

I blinked, chilled. I had assumed they wanted to take us captive and were just going about it inefficiently. To hear Toulon and his goons talking about killing us was something else. I mean, if he wanted to kill us, why not just shoot down the quadcopter? Even if we had crashed, why not strafe the wreckage of our quadcopter a few times? And if he did want to kill us, why take pictures of it? He was a billionaire industrialist, he wasn't a hitman gathering evidence that he had fulfilled his contract.

"Nah," said Toulon, taking another puff of his cigar. "Drag them out here. If I shoot them in the quadcopter, it will make for a terrible picture. I'll shoot them out here," he made a negligent gesture with his pistol, causing the bodyguards to take a prudent step back, "and then we'll get the pictures."

"Right," said another bodyguard, and he gestured. The three men started forward, Toulon hanging back as he concentrated on his cigar.

"That's it," muttered Tanner. "All of you, leave Toulon to me. I want to ask him a few questions. Take out the others." I nodded and took aim, sighting my Avenger on one of the approaching men. Tanner shifted, took a deep breath, and shouted.

"Now!" said Tanner. "Open up!"

He fired a single shot, and a half-second later the rest of us followed suit.

It happened fast, really fast, but at the time it felt like an agonized eternity. I had already sighted, my Avenger's barrel resting on a piece of twisted metal about the height of my chest, the stock braced against my shoulder, the iron sights at the end of the gun centered on one of the bodyguards. I squeezed the trigger, and the rifle bucked in my hands, the end of the weapon flashing. I hit the bodyguard on Toulon's right. I'm not sure where I hit him—either the upper chest or the right shoulder, but he staggered back. The expression of surprise on his face would have been comical under less grim circumstances. I fired again, and this time he spun around and fell.

Charles and Mr. Royale opened fire as well. The second bodyguard went down, his white shirt turning red with blood, and Toulon let out an astonished squawk, spun around, and collapsed, dropping both his pistol and his cigar. The final bodyguard turned to run, and either Charles or Mr. Royale caught him in the back of the leg.

The man fell, and as he did, he squeezed the trigger on his rocket launcher.

Mr. Royale barked a word that I had never heard him use before, and for an instant I was sure the rocket would blast us all to bits. Fortunately, the bodyguard fell over as he squeezed the trigger, and the launcher jerked in his hand, so instead of pointing at us, it was pointing over his shoulder.

That meant the rocket erupted from the launcher and slammed into the rear starboard rotor of Toulon's quadcopter. The rotor and a large part of the quadcopter's hull ripped itself apart in a raging fireball, shrapnel raining in all directions. I threw myself down, bits of metal bouncing off the wrecked quadcopter around me.

After a moment, the roar faded away, and all I could hear was the crackle of a fire.

"Anyone hurt?" barked Tanner.

"I report no injuries," said Charles.

"I'm fine," said Mr. Royale. "Sam?"

"I'm not hurt," I said. "Which, all things considered, is kind of surprising."

"Yeah," said Tanner, straightening up and peering outside again. "Let's have a little chat with Mr. Toulon, shall we?"

We stepped out of the quadcopter and into the jungle. Toulon's quadcopter was on fire. I had entertained a hope we could use it to fly back to Outpost Town, but the rocket had smashed one of the rotors and torn a big hole in the hull. The bodyguards were dead. Two of the men were dead from gunshot wounds, and the third had been killed by shrapnel from the explosion. Toulon himself lay on the ground, shivering, with gunshot wounds in his arm and leg, and a piece of shrapnel embedded in his side. That in itself probably would not be fatal, if he got to a doctor in time, but combined with the gunshots he was in trouble. Also there were all sorts of alien bacteria that would crawl into his open wounds, and the injections any visitor to Arborea received would only keep them at bay for so long.

He was in a lot of trouble. But to judge from the furious sneer he directed at us, the reality of his situation hadn't quite caught up with him yet.

"You're going to regret this," said Toulon, gritting his teeth. "You're going to pay, all of you."

"Yeah," said Tanner, pointing his Avenger at Toulon. "We're the ones bleeding to death in the middle of the Arborean jungle. We're the ones in trouble."

Toulon laughed. "Do you think Valier would let me die out here? I was one of his biggest backers for this plan, and I paid fifty million for this."

"Backers?" said Mr. Royale. "You weren't on the board of directors."

Again Toulon laughed. "Look, it's the burrito king. It would be fitting if you were ground up and served in your own disgusting burritos."

For a moment Mr. Royale just stared at him, and then he shook his head.

"I thought so. The Most Dangerous Game, I assume."

Toulon blinked. "You're not as stupid as you look."

"The Most Dangerous Game?" I said. "What is that?"

"The book I saw Valier reading," said Mr. Royale.

"So what does that have to do with anything?" I said.

"Everything. It was a book written by a man named Richard Connell on ancient Earth, long before even pre-interstellar spaceflight," said Mr. Royale. "In the story, a nobleman named Zaroff invites guests to his private island, where he hunts them for sport."

I looked at Toulon, at Mr. Royale, and then back at Toulon.

"Oh, man," I said. "That's really messed up."

"Seriously?" said Tanner. "The entire Safari Company is a…
a front so rich morons with too much money can hunt people
for sport?"

"Why would EcoMin allow something like that?" I said. "I
mean, I know they're scoundrels, but there's a big different
between corruption and graft and hunting people."

Toulon snorted. "The Acadarchy is broke. The only thing
that's keeping New Princeton afloat is loans from some of
the more solvent planetary governments, and they're getting
ready to pull the plug. So the Acadarchy needs money,
right? New Princeton is overpopulated anyway, and most
of the population consists of useless do-nothings. Why not
sell hunting rights to the highest bidder? Valier and his
pet ecocrats are on board with it, since they never shut up
about the negative effect mankind has on the interstellar ecology. Everybody wins. The Acadarchy gets a lot of money
to keep running, and they can get rid of some of their
surplus population. The customers get the thrill of a lifetime."

"Yeah, everyone wins," I said, "except for the people getting
hunted."

Toulon shrugged, sweat glittering on his face. "It's not like
you matter."

I kicked him. He let out a satisfying cry of pain, his
eyes going wide, and I wondered if he had ever been hit
before. Granted, kicking a wounded man when he's down
isn't the most chivalrous thing to do, but I figured he
deserved it. I might have kicked him again, or maybe
just shot him, but Tanner's free hand clamped over my
arm.

"None of that," said Tanner with the sort of hard smile he used when breaking up fights between rowdy workers. "Mr. Toulon is going to cooperate fully."

"And just why should I do that?" said Toulon.

"Because you've got nothing to lose," said Tanner, tapping his earpiece, "I've been recording everything since you strutted out of your quadcopter. And we're your only way out of the jungle."

"It doesn't matter what you've got," said Toulon. "Minister Valier himself supports this plan."

"Yeah," said Tanner, still with that nasty smile, "but he's not the only Minister, is he? And all the other Ministers hate his guts."

"This is true," said Mr. Royale. "The best way to deal with the Ecology Ministry, other than bribes, is to have friends in the other Ministries."

"Exactly," said Tanner. "And it's good to give friends a gift now and then. Such as a video that proves Valier set up his own private murder park on an alien world? See, the other Ministers might not care about that, but they do care about bringing down Valier, and my video is exactly the kind of club they can use against him. And against Toulon Group, too. I would bet Toulon Group has a lot of competitors, and I'm sure they'd love to have a PR weapon to use against it."

"Why, Winston," said Mr. Royale. "That was downright vicious."

"Thank you," said Tanner. "And if that doesn't persuade you, you're wounded, bleeding, and alone in the jungle. One of your hired idiots blew up your quadcopter, so you're stuck here. Unless you cooperate, you're not going anywhere."

"All right," said Toulon. "Fine! I'll admit to anything you want. Just get me back to Outpost Town."

I was sure that he was lying. If we took him back with us, he would spin some story for Valier that would get us all arrested and killed. Or Valier would simply have us executed to protect his secrets. A fresh wave of fear went through me. In the chaos of the crash, I hadn't been thinking about the explosion we had seen at Outpost Town. What about Kayla and Hoskins and the others? What had Valier and his men done to them?

"Security Director Tanner," said Charles. "We had better go now. All that blood will have drawn the notice of scavengers."

"You're right," said Tanner, grimacing. "All right. We'll need to work up some kind of sled for Toulon. It ought to be in the emergency supplies on one of the quadcopters…"

Then the scavengers in question showed up.

I spotted the first one lumbering towards us through the trees.

They didn't have a proper scientific name yet, or even a good nickname. We called them bears, because they sort of looked like the mammal from Old Earth, except that Terran bears did not have six legs, were not twenty feet long, and were not festooned with poisoned spikes down their spines. The Arborean bears were omnivores and lived on fungus and vegetation for the most part. That said, when they could get meat, they loved meat… and the smell of human blood seemed to draw them like flies to honey. They weren't as vicious or as cunning as the tromosaurs, but when roused, they were just as dangerous.

"Charles," said Tanner.

Charles raised his Avenger and got off three quick shots. His rounds penetrated the bear's head, and the creature went rigid and then collapsed, which allowed me to see the small troop of bears behind it.

For a moment they froze, staring at us. The bears looked a bit like a picture I had seen once, a freeze frame of a landslide right before it wiped out a village on some distant colony world.

I was pretty sure we were not the snow in this situation.

"What?" said Toulon. "What is it?"

"I advise immediate tactical retreat," said Charles.

"What are those things?" said Mr. Royale.

"Right," said Tanner. "We'll have to carry Toulon. Ian, you get his…"

The bears surged forward, and I had just enough time to reflect that they did rather look like an avalanche of spines and fur and large, sharp claws.

"Run!" shouted Charles.

"Wait! Wait!" said Toulon. "Please! Don't leave me!"

Even if we had wanted to, there was no way we could go back for him. The bears had the scent of the blood in their nostrils, and they were good and riled up. If we had hesitated even a second before running away, the bears would have ripped us apart as well.

It shouldn't have bothered me. Toulon had shot us down, murdered Hobson, and he would have gladly killed us all for trophies. But it still felt wrong.

A single shot rang out. Toulon fell silent.

As we sprinted away, I risked a glance over my shoulder. The bears tore into the three dead bodyguards, ripping them apart in a feeding frenzy. I didn't see Toulon, but I didn't hear him screaming either.

We kept running.

After about a mile, Charles called for a halt. We were all breathing hard.

"The bears will remain occupied with the dead until they are sated," said Charles, "and their scent should drive off any other predators. We should be safe for the moment." He paused and looked around the jungle, wiping sweat from his brow. "Within certain parameters of safety, you understand."

I looked at the other men. They were looking accusingly at Mr. Royale.

He shrugged. "I couldn't leave him to be devoured alive. That wouldn't have been right."

"He tried to kill us!" Tanner shouted. "Did you forget that?"

"It's one thing to shoot a man. Even he didn't intend for us to be torn apart by monsters."

"Only because that would spoil his trophies," I observed sourly.

"Regardless, Mr. Toulon is no longer the problem," said Mr. Royale. "I suggest we turn our attention to the situation at hand. What are we going to do now?"

That was a very good question, and I had no idea how to answer it.

Chapter 5

Interdepartmental Rivalries

"We're going back to Outpost Town," said Tanner. "Once we're there, we'll figure out what's going on, and then we'll make a plan of attack."

"Yeah," I said. "But when we get there, what are we going to do?"

"I don't know," said Tanner. "We'll figure it out then."

I started to say that wasn't a very good plan, but I made myself shut up. For one thing, it wouldn't have been helpful. That and Tanner had a point. We couldn't make a plan until we knew for sure what had happened at Outpost Town. Kayla was still at Outpost Town, which meant Tanner would stop at nothing to get her to safety.

"Very well," said Mr. Royale. "We had better get started. I presume we do not want to be caught outside in the jungle come nightfall."

"We do not," said Charles, who had never stopped surveilling our surroundings.

"Did you know?" said Tanner.

"Know what?" said Mr. Royale.

Tanner's mouth twisted. "What Safari Company was really about?"

"If I did know," said Mr. Royale, "Do you really think I would have let myself get on a quadcopter hunted by the likes of Alexander Toulon?"

"Good point," I said.

Mr. Royale shook his head. "I only invested in the Safari Company because it was New Princeton's first off-world business venture in decades. I hoped it might lead to restarting the colonization program. I had no idea it was a front for this sort of... sickness."

"What about all the sabotage, then?" I said.

"Sabotage?" said Charles.

Tanner scowled. "Do we really want to talk about this?"

Mr. Royale shrugged. "Why not? We're all in the same sinking ship at the moment."

"We were friends with Mr. Royale back on New Princeton," I told Charles. "That's why he hired us on. He was worried someone in the Ecology Ministry would try to sabotage the Safari Company, and he was right. I mean, didn't you ever wonder why so much stuff kept breaking down?"

"It is the nature of machinery to fail," said Charles. "Though we have had a high number of technical malfunctions."

"Yeah, a lot of those were on purpose," I said. "We'd get a shipment of cleanings drones and their cleaners would be pre-loaded with paint instead of bleach, or the harvesting drones had sabotaged drive units, stuff like that. Lots and lots of petty stuff. Most of it wasn't dangerous, but some of it could have hurt or killed someone."

"Or delayed the grand opening of Outpost Town," said Charles.

"I thought Valier supported the Safari Company," said Tanner, "and some faction within the Ministry opposed it."

Mr. Royale shrugged. "Maybe we were wrong. Maybe someone else is trying to stop the Safari Company."

"Or maybe," said Tanner, "we were right all along, but we had it backward."

"What do you mean?" said Charles.

"Right," said Tanner. "We assumed that Valier was in favor of Outpost Town and the Company and that some faction in the Ministry was trying to stop us because they don't think humans should affect the interstellar environment. But what if the faction in the Ministry was trying to stop Valier because they realized he's nuts?"

"Nuts?" I said.

"Obviously, Spraycan," said Tanner. "Hunting humans for sport and profit? That's the kind of thing that only happens on pirate asteroids in uncharted solar systems. New Princeton is a major power in the Thousand Worlds. It's supposed to be civilized." He added a mocking edge to the last word. "Something like this can't be kept secret forever. Sooner or later it will leak out, and there will be trouble. I bet Valier kept this secret from everyone else in the Acadarchy. I wasn't blowing smoke when I threatened Toulon. If that video gets out, the other Ministers would be delighted to tear Valier to shreds with this as an excuse."

I shuddered a little, thinking of how Toulon had been torn apart by the bears.

"Then that should be our plan of attack, Security Director Tanner," said Charles. "We must escape with proof of Minister Valier's misdeeds. Should we act quickly enough, he will fall to the other Ministers' attacks before he can bring down retribution upon our heads."

"And," said Mr. Royale, "we should try to rescue anyone we can from Outpost Town."

Charles scowled. "We should assume that all the guests are part of Valier's plot."

"We shouldn't," said Mr. Royale. "I'm not."

"Yes," said Tanner. "Apparently, Toulon found KwikBreets sufficiently offensive to kill you over them."

"Which is just appalling," said Mr. Royale. I expected him to say something about the morality of murder or the sanctity of human life, but I was wrong. "We use only the best ingredients in KwikBreets. The very best! And we have over twenty-nine different flavor configuration and styles."

"I thought it was twenty-seven," I said.

"We added two since you've been gone," said Mr. Royale. "Salsa and Spicy Buffalo Ranch. The second one is really quite popular, and has been our fifth bestseller–"

"My point," said Tanner, before Mr. Royale could get going, "is that all the guests might not be on Valier's side. This private murder park of his might be a way to raise money, but it's also a good way to settle some grudges. All those industrialists and traders who showed up for the grand opening brought their own bodyguards, and some of them might be on our side."

"We will not know until we can assess the situation further," said Charles.

"Like you said, Winston," said Mr. Royale. "I don't suppose we can call Outpost Town?"

"No such luck," said Tanner. "We can't get a radio signal back to Outpost Town without the boosters in the quadcopters. The vegetation mucks it up. That, and if Valier has control of the quadcopters, it's likely he'll send someone out to shoot us if he realizes that we got away from Toulon and his thugs."

"So we have to cross the jungle on foot," I said.

We stood in silence for a moment, contemplating that grim fact.

"It has been done before," said Charles.

"Never without casualties," I said.

"We don't have a choice," said Tanner. "Both quadcopters are wrecked, and if we call for help, we'll probably have Valier's goons show up to kill us. So unless one of you can magically grow a pair of wings or something, we're going to have to walk."

"The sooner we get moving," said Mr. Royale, "the sooner we can return and set matters right."

Or get ourselves shot, but I kept that thought myself.

"Exactly," said Tanner. "Let's get going. Charles, you've got the most experience with the jungle. You should take charge until we get back to Outpost Town."

"Very well, Security Director Tanner," said Charles, and he barked a stream of instructions.

Charles took point, with Tanner and Mr. Royale in the middle, and I brought up the back, which I usually did when I went out on hunting expeditions with Charles.

During the first five kilometers, we wound up shooting and killing about twenty-three tromosaurs. I wasn't sure if they were coming to investigate the wrecked quadcopters or not. The fire and the explosion would have frightened off most of the animals of the jungle, even the really big ones like the tankstriders, but as the fires died down the scent of blood from whatever remained of Toulon and his goons would have drawn scavengers and predators both. Sometimes the tromosaur packs followed the bears, hoping to steal away a bit of meat... or to take down an aging or a sick bear. The tromosaurs would kill anything if they could get away with it, and the things were clever.

We were careful. We had our sonic alarms ready on our wrists, and Charles led the way, dropping a pair of UV vision goggles over his eyes. The tromosaurs' stealth ability worked in both natural light and in infrared, probably because most of Arborea's animals could see into the infrared portions of the spectrum, but it was only partially effective in UV light.

The first pack of six tromosaurs came at us about two kilometers from the crash site. We activated our sonic alarms, and the tromosaurs hesitated long enough for us to start shooting. Tanner drilled two of them, and I got one. Mr. Royale and Charles accounted for the other three between them.

The next pack had nine tromosaurs, and that was a harder fight. We stood back to back, covering each other, and sending bursts of fire at the tromosaurs. The tromosaurs wavered, trying to decide to rush us or retreat, and Mr. Royale got two of them with bursts of full-auto. A third tromosaur almost got him, but I shot it through the head, so close that its blood spattered across my armor, and its carcass bounced off the ground about three inches in front of my boots, its mottled hide shifting through colors as it died.

"Good shot," said Mr. Royale, lowering his Avenger. "That one almost bit my head off."

"Thanks," I said, scanning the shadowed trees for more tromosaurs.

"You know," said Mr. Royale, "my accountant gave me all kinds of grief for the bribe I paid to keep you out of prison. I had no idea it would prove to be such an excellent investment."

"Well, if you kept me out of prison, it's only fair that I keep the tromosaurs from eating you," I said. "Where did you learn to shoot? It's obvious you've handled a gun before."

"I served in the Security Ministry for a year when I was your age," said Mr. Royale.

Tanner grunted. "Really? Only a year? What happened?"

Mr. Royale smiled. "I was drummed out for selling liquor on the side to Security Ministry officers. It would have been a more serious charge, but the commander of my department was very fond of wine from the orbital vineyards, and I found it for him cheap." He tapped the stock of the Avenger. "Fortunately, some the skills I acquired during that year remain useful to this day."

"Yes, business on the side," said Tanner. "That how we ended up here."

"Now, now, Winston," said Mr. Royale. "The whole point of developing useful skills like yours is to hire them out to people like me."

Tanner grunted, and we kept moving through the jungle. Two more tromosaur packs came after us in the space of the next three kilometers, but we managed to fight through them. As annoying as it had been to carry all those extra supplies and ammunition, I was glad that Charles had been such a martinet about it.

After killing the fourth tromosaur pack, we had to divert to avoid a tankstrider as the huge creature lumbered through the jungle, eating the foliage and fungus growing on the lower levels of the massive trees. The tankstrider wouldn't attack us unless we provoked it, but it might not notice that we were there, and it was entirely possible that the huge animal would trample us without even realizing it. Pity we couldn't convince the tromosaurs to go after it, but the tromosaurs would only attack wounded or dying tankstriders, and even then more often than not the tankstrider won the fight.

"Big fellows, aren't they?" said Mr. Royale as the tankstrider lumbered off into the jungle. The ground vibrated a little with every step. "Pity we can't just ride it back to Outpost Town."

"That is inadvisable, Board Member Royale," said Charles. "Do you see the moss and other fungi growing up the animal's back? There are any number of parasitic herbivores that subsist upon them."

Mr. Royale shrugged. "Herbivores aren't a problem."

"No," said Tanner, pointing at a flying dark shape that flitted after the tankstrider, "it's the things that eat the herbivores that are the problem. The tankstriders have their own little mobile ecosystem around them. It…"

The sound of the explosion cut him off.

My head snapped around, my Avenger coming up on reflex. I didn't see anything unusual, but the sound of an explosion had been unmistakable… and in the distance, I saw the sudden glare of firelight. The noise was so loud that the departing tankstrider even paused for a second before it resumed its leisurely course in search of food.

"That," I said, "sounded a lot like a quadcopter crash."

"Yeah," said Tanner, and he shared a look with Charles. "More of Valier's games?"

"Most probably," said Charles. "Best to go around it, I think, and continue to Outpost Town."

Mr. Royale frowned. "There might be survivors."

"They might also have been killed in the crash," said Tanner, "and there are probably another group of hunters like Toulon and his goons coming for a landing right now."

"It is also possible we will find allies," said Mr. Royale. "Quite a few quads left on tours at the same time we did, probably so Valier could send out his first round of hunters. If the pilots and guides upon those quads are as thorough as Senior Guide Charles…"

"They better have been," said Charles.

"Then they will also be armed," said Mr. Royale. "We could recruit ourselves a militia, as it were."

Tanner snorted. "Well, Spraycan, what do you think?"

I blinked. He didn't often ask for my opinion.

"I think we should look for survivors," I said. "And if more hunters return, we can help fight them off. If we do that, they'll be more willing to help us."

Tanner sighed. "Yeah, you're probably right. And if Kayla knew I passed someone by who needed help, she'd never let me hear the end of it. All right. Charles, take point. Let's check out the crash."

We moved as fast as we did through the alien underbrush of the Arborean jungle, Charles taking the lead. I swept my eyes back and forth, seeking for any signs of tromosaurs or other predators. The crash would have scared them off, at least for now, but if there were wounded or dying or dead men near the wreckage, eventually the smell of blood would draw the predators. The glow of the fire got brighter, and I could smell the crash, a mixture of burning fuel and heated metal and scorched electronics…

Gunshots rang out.

Reflexes took over, and I threw myself to the ground, the others following suit. The sound of more gunshots rolled through the jungle, followed by the dull boom of something I thought was a bomb or a grenade or maybe another handheld rocket launcher like the one that Toulon's bodyguard had used.

"Get up," said Tanner, rising to his feet. "It's still a distance off, and I don't think it's aimed at us."

"A battle," said Mr. Royale, grunting as he stood.

"Yeah," said Tanner. "Looks like one of Valier's hunters is encountering resistance."

Charles frowned with disapproval. "Failure to respect the animals in a hunt is a cardinal error."

"There is a reason that book called humans the most dangerous game," said Mr. Royale.

"Looks like you were right about allies, Ian," said Tanner. "Let's go. Charles, keep us under cover if possible. And keep a lookout for tromosaurs. The gunfire and the smoke should keep them scared off, but I wouldn't want to trust my life to that."

I nodded and followed the others. Charles led us in a zigzag path, ducking from massive tree to massive tree while the light of the fire grew brighter and the sound of gunfire got louder. Then Charles ducked behind another tree, and I saw the fighting ahead.

One of Safari Company's quadcopters had crashed hard into the ground ahead, digging up a deep furrow in the earth. Fires danced in the smashed quadcopter's canopy, though it hadn't exploded. About thirty yards from the wreck sat an intact Avionics AA-39 quadcopter, identical to the one that Toulon had used. A group of men had taken cover in the crash furrow, using it as an impromptu trench, sometimes rising slightly to fire off a few rounds. Six men in body armor crouched near the Avionics quadcopter, sending volleys of fire towards the furrow.

"I know him," muttered Mr. Royale.

"Who?" said Tanner.

"The man leading those hunters," said Mr. Royale. "His name is Philip Lysokos. He's another billionaire. The Lysokos Company is based in the Silure star system, manufactures hyperdrives. He sells hyperdrives to half the governments and militaries in the Thousand Worlds."

"Is there some sort of secret billionaire club?" I said. "Like they all got together one day and decided to go hunt their fellow man for sport?"

"Yeah, and Valier founded the club," said Tanner. "I think we can take them. Ian, you recognize the guys in the furrow?"

"Maybe," said Mr. Royale. "I'm not sure… but I think they're wearing Security Ministry uniforms."

I blinked, and then the memory came back. "That colonel who rode over on your ship… um, what was his name?"

"Colonel Cassius Argent," said Mr. Royale. "I think those are his men." He frowned. "If he knew anything about this and didn't tell me, I'll be disappointed in him."

"Then he'll owe you twice over," said Tanner. "Once, for not telling you, and again when we save his life right now. Pick your targets." Neither side in the gunfight had noticed us yet, and we took aim.

"Are we shooting to kill?" I said.

"Yes," said Tanner, his voice hard.

I hesitated. I had never actually killed someone in cold blood. I mean, I had helped kill Toulon's bodyguards, but that had been in the heat of the fight, and they had been trying to kill us. Still, Lysokos and his goons deserved it. Presumably, Lysokos had spent millions of credits for the right to hunt down and kill innocent people, and his bodyguards had gone along with it. Maybe they deserved to get killed. That, and I knew they would kill us if given a chance.

"Right," I said.

"On three," said Tanner, and he settled into a firing stance, aiming his Avenger. No one had noticed us. That was about to change.

Tanner finished counting off, and we started shooting.

It was almost ridiculously easy. Not that I'm complaining about that, mind you. Lysokos and his men were focused on their opponents in the furrow and still hadn't realized that we were there. All four of us hit on our first shots, sending the men tumbling to the ground. I shifted aim, firing again at the two men still on their feet, and they went down in a hail of bullets as the others fired again.

For a moment silence fell over the jungle, save for the crackle of flames in the downed quadcopter.

"Who's there?" called a rough voice from the furrow.

"I'm Winston Tanner," called Tanner. "Security Director for Safari Company. One of Minister Valier's guests shot down our quadcopter, and we've been trying to make our way back to Outpost Town to find out what's going on."

The voice laughed, and a head and pair of shoulders rose over the rough edge of earth, and I recognized the scarred features of Colonel Cassius Argent. "That so? There are all sorts of unpleasant surprises today, Tanner."

"So I gathered," said Mr. Royale.

"That you, Royale?" said Argent. "I'm relieved you're not involved in this mess."

"Not involved?" said Mr. Royale. "I'm stranded in the Arborean jungle."

"Let me rephrase that," said Argent. "I'm glad you're not responsible for this mess. If you were, you wouldn't be stranded in the Arborean jungle."

"You knew this was going to happen, and you didn't warn me?" said Mr. Royale. "People have died, Colonel."

"If we had known how far along Minister Valier's plans were, we would have taken action," said Argent. "But we had no idea!"

Both Mr. Royale and Argent began trying to talk over each other.

"Okay, okay, okay," said Tanner. "All right. It looks like we're on the same side, right? So let's keep the quarreling to a minimum, and put all our cards on the table. We're going to come out from cover. If we do that, do you promise not to shoot us?"

"Fine," said Argent.

He straightened up, stepping out of the furrow, his black uniform smudged with blood and dust. There was a nasty cut on his temple, one that would likely make a new addition to his collection of scars. He was carrying a rifle of a design I did not recognize, probably Security Ministry standard issue. Two of his men followed him. I wondered what had happened to the other two who had accompanied him on Mr. Royale's ship, and then realized that they had probably died in the crash or in the firefight.

"Mulger, stay with me," said Argent. "Thompkins, go check Lysokos and his men. Make sure they're not playing dead."

One of his men went to check on the men lying dead on the ground. Argent and Mulger walked towards us, rifles held low, but their fingers still rested near their triggers.

"So," said Argent. "How did you wind up taking a stroll through the jungle today?"

"We were taking a tour through the jungle," said Mr. Royale. "One of those EcoMin special ops quads came up behind us, ignored our calls, and shot us down. Our pilot was killed in the crash. The EcoMin quad was carrying Alexander Toulon and his bodyguards, and when they landed, they tried to kill us."

"Toulon?" said Argent, blinking. "Toulon was dumb enough to get wrapped up in all of this? Makes sense, I suppose. He was always one of Valier's cronies." He craned his neck. "Since I don't see Toulon, I assume you killed him."

"Not exactly," said Tanner. "A large park of local omnivores with a preference towards carrion arrived at the crash site, drawn by the scent of blood, and we were forced to retreat before we were overwhelmed."

"And Toulon just happened to get eaten, is that it?" said Argent. "Along with his men."

"Afraid so," said Tanner.

Argent snorted. "I feel sorry for the creature that ate that man. No man that poisonous is going to sit well in anything's belly."

"That's our story," said Tanner. "So how did you wind up taking a walk through the jungle?"

Thompkins finished his inspection of the dead men and rejoined the colonel.

"I suspect our story is about the same as yours," said Argent. "Valier invited the guests to take a tour of the local jungle via quadcopter. It seemed like a good method of reconnaissance, so we went up with one of your pilots. We had only gotten about twenty kilometers away from Outpost Town when that thing," he waved his gun at the Avionics quadcopter, "turned up on our tail. I thought Valier had dispatched some EcoMin operators to shoot us down, but as it turned out, it was a hyperdrive magnate with some overpriced and incompetent bodyguards." His grim face turned harder. "Two of my men and our pilot died in the crash. I won't forgive that."

"I assume," said Tanner, "that you were here to investigate Valier?"

"You are correct," said Argent. "The Ecology Ministry has long held an excessive influence over politics on New Princeton."

"There's an understatement," I said.

Argent blinked and me and kept speaking. "So investigating the Ecology Minister is a politically difficult challenge, even though Valier has a long list of crimes and misdeeds and outright felonies to his name."

"I've heard of a few of them," said Tanner, his voice flat. I assumed he was thinking of Kayla and the pesticide that had left her sterile.

"Unfortunately, Valier is clever, an immensely gifted politician, and as slippery as a greased rail," said Argent. "Seemingly airtight prosecutions against him have collapsed twice to my knowledge, because he was willing to bribe or coerce witnesses, and because he was able to call in favors."

"Yeah," said Tanner in a dry voice. "I've heard that."

"The Security Ministry," said Argent, "has wished to bring Valier down for a considerable time. His sudden interest in the Safari Company project captured our attention, because it was so out of character for him."

"Why?" I said. "He's a crook. Crooks do sleazy things. Like hunting people for sport."

"Valier's a crook," said Argent, "but as far as we can tell, he really believes EcoMin's official line. He believes that mankind is a blight on the interstellar environment, that human populations need to be culled and regulated, and that we should not colonize any new worlds."

"So if he really believes that," I said, "then why is he a crook?"

Mr. Royale snorted. "Because he thinks he's doing righteous work, Sam. And since he's doing righteous work, he feels justified in enriching himself along the way. But the Thousand Worlds would be a happier place if we each tended to our own concerns rather than running around trying to improve everyone else."

"We should move on," said Charles. "It is best not to linger here. The odor of burning fuel will mask our scents for a while, but sooner or later the tromosaurs and other predators will follow the scent of blood."

"Right," said Tanner. "We'd better decide what to do, Colonel."

"Agreed," said Argent. "Perhaps it would be better to continue this discussion once we have reached a place of greater safety."

"I might have an idea about that," said Tanner, looking at the dead men. "One of Toulon's goons accidentally shot his quadcopter with a rocket launcher."

Argent frowned. "Seriously?"

"Afraid so," I said.

"We had to walk," said Tanner, turning towards Lysokos's quadcopter. "Was this thing damaged at all?"

"Not to my knowledge," said Argent. "Lysokos shut it down when he landed."

"We don't have a pilot," I said.

"I've seen you fly drones," said Tanner.

"That's different," I said.

Mulger raised a hand. "I'm certified on a patrol quadcopter. This is a little bigger than I'm used to, but if our other option is to cross ten kilometers of jungle, I am willing to try."

"Lysokos might have locked the quadcopter," said Mr. Royale. "Sometimes the EcoMin quads require encrypted keys to unlock the controls."

"True," said Tanner. "Fortunately, Lysokos is dead, so I don't think he'll complain too loudly if we take his stuff."

"Then I suggest," said Mr. Royale, "that we continue this conversation in flight."

We paused long enough to loot the corpses of Lysokos and his men for weapons and ammunition, and to look for the encryption keys. When Mr. Royale mentioned them, I thought it had been a file stored on an external drive or something. It turned out it was a big metal key with a black flat head. Evidently, the encryption key was stored within the key's head. I admit that looting the corpses felt ghoulish, but since Lysokos was the same kind of murderous freak looking for kicks as Toulon, I didn't feel too guilty about it.

Once we finished, we boarded the quadcopter, making sure to close and lock the doors behind us, which made us marginally safer. The tromosaurs were clever enough to find a way inside if given enough time, though hopefully we would be in the air before that happened... or before a passing tankstrider happened to flatten us on its way to sample some promising foliage.

Mulger took the pilot's seat, and I settled into the co-pilot's chair, blinking at the controls. Tanner, Mr. Royale, Charles, Argent, and Thompkins took the passenger cabin behind us.

"Right," said Mulger. "What do you think?"

"Hmm," I said, looking over the controls. "I wish Hobson was still alive to do this."

"What?" said Mulger.

"Never mind," I said. I had flown some of the Safari Company's aerial drones, so I knew the basics. Of course, the difference between a flight drone and a quadcopter was like the difference between a popgun and a rocket launcher. Hopefully, Mulger knew what he was doing. "All right. Let's see. There, the console's unlocked now, and I'll start the preflight check on the engines."

Mulger nodded and started flipping switches. More lights blinked to life on the control board, and I heard a whine as the engines started up. I checked the pressure levels, the fuel flow, the temperatures, and the rotor status, and everything came up green. Maybe it wasn't that much different from repairing Uncle Morgan's autonomous tractors after all.

"So," said Tanner from the passenger cabin. I listened with half an ear as I went through the rest of the preflight checklist. "Since we're waiting to take off, you might as well tell us the rest of the story."

"Very well," said Argent. "As I said, the Security Ministry has been after Valier for a long time. Recently, however, the political situation on New Princeton has made his position precarious."

"Political situation?" said Charles.

"The Acadarchy is broke," said Mr. Royale. "They've been running a deficit for decades, and no one will lend them money."

"Correct," said Argent. "The money has just about run out. Simply put, there are drastic changes coming to New Princeton, and a lot of things are going to have to be cut. The Ecology Ministry is powerful, but it doesn't bring in any revenues. They have simply run out of businesses to fine. So to save his career and his power, Valier needs another source of revenue, and fast."

"Hence the Safari Company," said Tanner.

"The technical legal term in interstellar law for what Valier is attempting to set up on Arborea is 'interstellar human trafficking for purposes of sport-based homicide'," said Argent.

"Something of a mouthful," said Mr. Royale.

"Indeed," said Argent. "Unfortunately, that mouthful is depressingly common. Societies tend to develop a taste for blood sports in their declining stages, and there are an abundance of people with more money than scruples. This kind of thing tends to happen often in interstellar space, in places where no government or NGO holds sway. Refurbished asteroid mines, abandoned space stations, derelict ice tankers, and so forth. A client can visit a place like that and buy people to do whatever he wants to them. Hunting them for sport is one of the more popular options. What Valier is trying to do here is simply that on a larger and more extravagant scale."

"How are the fuel pumps?" said Mulger.

"Looking good," I said, looking at the control panel. I wanted to listen to Tanner's conversation with Argent, but I decided it was probably a higher priority to help Mulger make sure we didn't crash. "Green."

"Good," said Mulger. He raised his voice. "Strap in, people. We are taking off."

He began flipping switches, and the whine of the engines grew louder.

"So, let's hear it," said Tanner, "Do you have a plan or not?"

"I have a plan," said Argent. "And I'll need your help."

Mulger gripped the throttles, and the quadcopter shivered, lifting from the ground and into the air, turning slowly as it gained altitude.

"Watch out for the trees," I said. "If we hit one of those big branches it'll shear the blades right off the propellers."

"Right," said Mulger. "I think we'll head up through gaps in the layers until we get through the top canopy."

"I'll watch the radar and the cams," I said, flipping switches to bring up the displays.

"Once we clear the canopy, we'll head back to Outpost Town," said Mulger.

And then what?

I kept my eye on the radar and camera screen, listening as Argent explained his plan to Tanner.

"Our orders were to investigate Valier's plans on Arborea," said Argent, "and to take action if necessary."

"If you wanted to take action," said Tanner, "you should have brought more than five men."

"I did," said Argent. "I landed planetside on Royale's ship. What we didn't mention to anyone is that a Security Ministry gunship followed us into the system."

"How many men are on that ship?" said Mr. Royale.

"Not counting the crew, seventy-five combat officers," said Argent. "All of them equipped with battle armor. The gunship's armaments include a full complement of space-to-ground missiles as well as orbital artillery. If need be, we can take over Outpost Town with minimal casualties."

"Minimal casualties," said Tanner. "To yourselves? Or to the Safari Company personnel?"

"Both, I hope. But given that Valier plans to hunt Safari personnel for sport, I'd say that minimal casualties is at this point the best case scenario for the company."

"Fine," said Tanner. "So we call up your friends and deal with Valier."

"There is our difficulty," said Argent. "Because of the political sensitivity of coming after the Ecology Minister, it was vitally important that no one knew the gunship was here. The gunship entered via the outer system and is currently parked in a high orbit behind Arborea's moon."

"Which is well out of the range of any handheld communication devices," said Charles.

"Right," said Argent. "The plan was that I would land, take a look around, and communicate to the gunship if any action was needed. Unfortunately, we didn't realize that Valier's plans were so far advanced."

"So you need a transmitter strong enough to reach to your men on the ship," said Tanner. "Which means breaking into the communications room in the administrative building at Outpost Town, and that is now almost certainly in the hands of Valier and his men."

"You summarize the problem admirably well," said Argent.

"Spraycan!" said Tanner. "Is there any way we can rig up a transmitter? Something powerful enough to reach the ship?"

"What?" I said, trying to concentrate on the displays as Mulger eased the quadcopter up. We were five hundred feet off the ground by now, but the branches were no less thick. "No. Probably not. We don't have the right equipment. Arborea's magnetic field is too powerful, and you need a pretty powerful transmitter to punch through it and get past the atmosphere."

"So you need better equipment," said Mr. Royale.

"Yes," said Argent. "Specifically, we need to use the equipment in Outpost Town's communications room to control the communications satellite Safari Company put in orbit to hail incoming ships. With that, we can contact the gunship and call for reinforcement. However many EMSO agents Valier has with him, they won't be able to deal with seventy-five Security Ministry officers in battle armor."

"Let's hope not," said Tanner.

"Where exactly is the communications room?" said Mr. Royale.

"In the administrative center, not far from Hoskins' office," said Tanner. "Valier and his men have probably taken over the building."

"He did not bring that many men with him," said Charles.

Tanner snorted. "He didn't need to bother. That's why he sent us all out on tours for the VIPs. Every single guide can handle weapons, and every single guide went up in the quads. We were the first round of victims for the biggest hunt of the century. Clever. He satisfies his first round of customers, wipes out the most dangerous opposition, and kills off any witnesses. Three birds in one."

I wondered if Valier had slaughtered the Safari Company employees back at Outpost Town. Maybe he had kept them alive as captives. Or maybe he would drive them into the jungle for the second round of hunts.

"That is the most likely case," said Argent. "This is our best chance to act, to save as many lives as possible, and to catch Valier with so much evidence against him that even he will not be able to wriggle out of the consequences this time. I suggest we return to Outpost Town, land the quad, and try to get into the comms room undetected."

"That's all, huh?" said Tanner. "You make it sound simple."

"It's very simple," said Argent. I glanced back at Argent long enough to see the smile on his scarred face. "But simple isn't the same as easy."

"No," said Tanner. "Spraycan! How we doing?"

I examined the radar display. "We're just about through the last layer of the forest…"

Brilliant sunlight poured through the quadcopter's canopy, and I blinked a few times to clear my eyes. We were hovering over the top of the highest branches of the jungle, the leaves sway beneath us in the wind from our rotors.

"So I see," said Argent. "Mulger, take us back to Outpost Town."

"Yes, sir," said Mulger, and he turned the quadcopter around, flying over the jungle below.

Chapter 6
Complications

Once, a few weeks after I started working at Outpost Town, I asked Charles why he always over-prepared for hunting expeditions. I meant it as a joke, but back then I hadn't realized that Hiram Charles did not actually have a sense of humor, and I got an earnest twenty-minute lecture for my trouble.

"Preparation is essential in all matters, Indentured Worker Hammond," said Charles. "This is especially true in the jungle, where all forms of life have no fear of humans and most of the predators are eager to attack us. There we must prepare ourselves for all contingencies. Of course, we cannot anticipate every single thing that might go wrong, but the more thoroughly we prepare, the greater resources we have at our disposal for adapting to unexpected difficulties."

I didn't know if Charles was religious or not, but I strongly suspected his gods were Preparedness, Vigilance, and Diligence, and he served them as devotedly as any man ever served a deity. Given how often they had saved his life, it was hard to blame him.

Right about then, however, EcoMin's lack of preparedness bit us, and bit us hard.

I don't think Paul Valier had someone like Hiram Charles to advise him. If he had, he could have easily avoided a lot of problems. In all my interactions with Ecology Ministry people, I had noticed that they were not very good at actually getting things done. Sure, they were highly educated. Sure, they had a lot of degrees. Theresa's mom had three herself. Her house had two bathrooms, and when I had first started seeing Theresa, she and her mother had constantly been fighting because the toilet was broken in one of them, and both Theresa and her mother needed a lot of time getting ready in the morning. The toilet had been broken for months, and neither Theresa nor her mother knew how to fix it or had even gotten around to arranging for someone to fix it. I repaired it in about an hour, and the sudden reduction in mother-daughter strife was probably the reason Theresa's mother hadn't tried to make her break up with me even sooner.

I suppose fixing that stupid toilet caused me a lot of trouble in the end.

So, the ecocrats weren't that great on practical matters, or at thinking things through, which I realized when the radar display suddenly lit up with multiple contacts.

"Hey," said Mulger, tearing his eyes from the canopy for a moment. He was doing a good job of flying the quadcopter, but I could tell it was a strain. "Those aren't missiles, are they?"

"No, too slow," I said, staring at the display. About thirty different radar contacts had risen from the forest about a kilometer to the west and were heading right for us. I have a lot of useful skills, but I didn't know how to read a radar display beyond the basics. Nevertheless, I was pretty sure what they were. "Hey, Tanner, Charles? I think you'd better look at this."

Tanner grunted and heaved himself out of the seat, standing behind the co-pilot's chair, and Charles joined him a second later.

"This is a problem," said Charles.

"Why? What is it?" said Argent. "Those don't look like missiles or combat drones."

"They're aerials, aren't they?" I said.

"Aerials?" said Mulger. "Like flying antennas?"

"No," I said. "Much worse."

"Flying predators," said Charles. "Roughly equivalent to reptiles. They are quite strong and aggressive, and furthermore breathe a corrosive liquid that can even eat through reinforced metal, such as the armored hull of the quadcopter."

Mulger said several bad words as the formation of aerials drew closer.

"They are easy to evade," said Charles. "A simple chemical concoction repels they. We need only deploy that."

"Yeah," I said, looking at the lights and displays on the panel. "I don't think this thing is equipped with a sprayer system. Do you see one?"

"What?" said Charles, quickly looking around the instruments. "This vehicle is not equipped with a chemical spraying system. Outrageous! What sort of idiot planned this expedition?" He sounded more offended by the oversight than the fact that the aerials would try to rip apart the quadcopter to eat us.

"Will they attack us?" said Argent.

"Most likely," said Tanner. "That acidic cocktail they spit out can chew through the hull and start fires. Once we crash, they'll peel open the hull, and eat us after we're good and cooked."

"Cooked?" said Argent.

"The acid breath," said Charles. "They do not prefer to eat their meat raw."

Argent shook his head. "This planet. Can we get away from them?"

"We should be able to," said Charles. "What is the altitude ceiling on this vehicle?"

"Uh," said Mulger. "I… don't actually know." He tapped a control, and a system readout came to life on one of the displays. "Looks like… two and a half kilometers."

"Excellent," announced Charles. "The aerials never ascend to higher than two or three hundred meters above the top of the jungle canopy. We merely need to climb above their range, and they won't be able to follow. Eventually they will lose interest in us."

"Sounds like a plan," said Argent. "Do it, Mulger."

"Sir," said Mulger. He pulled a lever, and the roar of the rotors grew louder as the engines kicked to maximum, various gauges on my control panel inching towards the red. I felt the acceleration pressing me into the copilot's seat, and I heard Tanner grunt as he shifted position to brace against the acceleration. The position of the contacts on the radar displayed started to change, and while I wasn't sure what I was looking at, I nevertheless thought that the position of the aerials was changing relative to our position. That meant they were staying at the same height while we were flying higher.

At least, I hoped that was what it meant.

"I think it's working!" said Mulger, flipping some more switches. Even with our earpieces, he had to shout to make himself heard over the howl of the engines. "Some of them are following us, but they aren't coming any higher and it looks like they're beginning to lose interest."

"Head towards Outpost!" said Tanner.

"Won't they just follow us?" said Argent.

"They may," said Charles, "but the HVAC systems of the buildings of Outpost Town regularly emit a burst of the repelling chemical. The aerials will not follow us inside the perimeter."

"Head in a high arc towards Outpost Town," said Argent. "We can descend and put down in the cleared area around the town."

Thompkins scowled. "We will be vulnerable to the town's anti-aircraft defenses. If Valier's men are manning them, they'll bring us down."

"Outpost Town doesn't have any anti-aircraft defenses," said Tanner. "EcoMin wouldn't allow it when they authorized this place. I suppose Valier didn't want any of his victims fighting back."

"Anti-aircraft defenses aren't cheap," observed Mr. Royale. "I expect they blew most of their budget on the anti-monster defenses."

"I don't see that we have any choice, gentlemen," said Argent. "If we descend towards the canopy and land in the jungle, those aerial things will swarm us. Our best course is to descend in an arc from our current altitude and into the airspace over Outpost Town."

"I would rather put down in the jungle a kilometer or so from Outpost Town," said Tanner. "We could make our way on foot to Outpost Town undetected, and it would be easier to traverse a kilometer of the tromosaur-infested jungle than fifteen."

Argent shrugged. "If the aerials stop following us, perhaps we can try it."

"Looks like about ten have decided to stay with us," said Mulger, tapping the radar display.

"Guess that settles that," said Tanner.

We flew in silence for a while, save for the roar of the engines. After a few moments, the coast and the ocean came into sight and the expanse of cleared space around Outpost Town. I saw the buildings of the town, the rows of spacecraft parked on the landing field glinting in the sunlight.

"All right," said Argent. "Mulger, start putting us down. Gentle arc. Set us down somewhere at the edge of the sonic fence, and…"

A shrill electronic tone cut into the cabin, and red lights began flashing on the control panels.

"What is that?" said Mr. Royale.

"Radar lock!" said Thompkins.

"Someone's painted us with a targeting laser, too," said Mulger. "Based on the signal strength, I'd say it's a man-portable rocket launcher. Sir, we'd better…"

The alarm got shriller, and the word INCOMING DETECTED appeared on one of the displays.

"Incoming!" said Thompkins. "Looks like two heat-seekers."

"Going evasive!" said Mulger, sending the quadcopter spiraling towards the jungle below.

"The aerials will be all over us," said Charles.

"They might, but the missiles will kill us a lot quicker," said Argent. "Get us down into the trees, quickly. That might confuse their homing systems."

Mulger sent the quadcopter diving towards the canopy, and two things caught my attention. The first was the gray-green shapes of the aerials flying below us. The big animals looked like a twisted combination of a mythical Terran dragon, a blimp, and a hot water bottle. They were big animals, each one about the size of a car, with wingspans of over twenty feet, their scaled hides a mottled, glistening, greenish-gray. Despite their bulk, they weren't that heavy, comparatively. Their bloated, sausage-like bodies held enormous bladders of lighter-than-air gas. Evidently, something in their metabolism produced the stuff naturally, allowing them to fly, and also providing the acidic breath they could breathe from their fanged mouths.

And Mulger's evasive course was going to take us right through them.

The second thing I noticed was the flare of fire rising over Outpost Town, a flare of fire that drew nearer with every heartbeat. As it drew closer, I realized that it was two plumes of fire rising from the end of a pair of missiles hurtling towards us.

Somehow, we made it through the flyers without any of them breathing on us. I think our abrupt descent might have scared them a little, because they scattered in every direction as we plunged through them. But they recovered quickly, turned around, and began to come after us again.

"Does this thing have any countermeasures?" said Argent. "Flares or chaff?"

"No, sir," said Mulger, accelerating into the dive. "Crash positions!"

The others scrambled into their seats, making sure their straps were secure.

"Brace for impact!" said Mulger. "I don't think we can avoid both missiles."

"Then we're dead," I said, despair settling over me.

"Not necessarily," said Mulger, his eyes hard upon the controls and the display. "They aren't big enough to hold a large warhead."

The proximity alarm shrilled louder, and at the last minute, Mulger spun the quadcopter at full speed. The engines howled in protest, and the fuselage gave off an alarming shriek of stressed metal.

One of the missiles slammed into the starboard side of the quadcopter.

The explosion shook the quadcopter like a child's toy, and if I hadn't been strapped in, the shock would have thrown me into the wall. All kinds of alarms started blaring and flashing on the control panels, and Mulger snarled and started flipping switches.

"Shut down the aft starboard rotor!" he shouted. "It's drawing fuel, and it's on fire."

I flipped the kill switches, and some of the engine noise subsided. The quadcopter gave an alarming lurch as it descended, and I risked a look at the central systems display. Mulger had been right. I had feared the missile would rip apart the quadcopter, but the warhead wasn't big enough to do that. It had taken out the aft rear rotor, but the quadcopter was still flying on its three remaining rotors.

But I feared it wouldn't be for much longer. The missile lock alarm still blared, and through the winds, I saw that both the aerials and the jungle canopy were much closer.

The quadcopter had lost a lot of its altitude. Worse, it had lost speed. From what I remembered of the technical manuals Charles had made me read, the quadcopter could still fly with two functional rotors, and with one functional rotor it could, with luck, manage a mostly controlled landing but not much else. With three rotors it could stay flying, albeit slower and less maneuverable. Under normal circumstances, that wouldn't have been a problem.

With a pack of hungry aerials in pursuit and one more missile on our tails, that was another matter.

"Second missile incoming," said Mulger. "Hammond, on my mark, cut power to the port fore rotor."

I started to protest, realized I didn't know what I was talking about, and nodded.

Mulger glared at the radar display, the flashing dot of the second missile looping around to head towards us. "Three... two... one... now! Now!"

I cut the engine, and the quadcopter gave an alarming lurch as Mulger yanked the controls, spinning the craft into the path of the missile. This time, I saw the fireball as the blast ripped apart the forward port rotor and sent flaming debris tumbling past the canopy.

An instant later we plunged through the top of the forest and back into the Arborean jungle. Forget the aerials, now gravity was the more immediate danger.

"Hang on!" shouted Mulger. "We're going down!"

I said several bad words, and I heard the roar and felt the thrum through the deck as Mulger opened up with every single one of the quadcopter's weapons at once. There was a snapping, tearing sound, followed by a disturbing crunching noise, and then a hideous whine from the engines as they started to fail.

"Brace yourselves!" said Mulger. "Impact in three, two, one..."

There was an almighty grinding sound, and then the quadcopter heaved, the impact shooting through every bone in my body at once. I slammed into my restraints so hard that I felt like my gut was about to rupture, and then I was thrown back into my seat once again.

Slowly, the grinding noise faded to nothing, and the quad-copter came to a halt.

Silence and smoke filled the cabin, accompanied by the smell of something burning.

"All right, look alive," said Tanner, though he sounded a bit wobbly. He started unstrapping. "Check in, people. Anyone hurt?"

"I'm fine," said Mulger.

"Also fine," said Thompkins.

Argent, Charles, and Mr. Royale were all uninjured as well. I hadn't been expecting that. Hobson hadn't made it out of the last crash alive. I thought about how unlikely it was that I had been in two quadcopter crashes in the same day, and decided not to think about it further. I had probably already used up my entire lifetime's allocation of luck, and I was going to need a lot more luck to get out of Paul Valier's crazy hunt alive.

On the other hand, maybe I had more than my fair share of luck. It was just bad luck.

"You were firing on the way down," said Argent, squinting at his two men. "Why?"

Mulger shrugged. "We couldn't use the guns against those balloon-bird things, whatever they're called…"

"Aerials," said Charles.

"Right, aerials," said Mulger. "So I figured we could use them to clear a path down for us, shoot some holes in all those branches so we didn't smash up against a tree." He scratched at his jaw. "Guess it worked, seeing as how we're still alive. Didn't it turn out so well for the quadcopter, though."

"I'm sure the Ecology Ministry can lodge a complaint with the Security Ministry," said Mr. Royale. "Although I doubt they have a form for this particular situation."

"You might be surprised. But they'll have a lot more to complain about before we're done," said Argent, reaching for his belt.

I heard a distant screech from high overhead. The aerials were making their way through the canopy, following us down, and I really didn't want to be caught inside the wrecked quadcopter when they found us.

"We should go," I said.

"Yes," said Tanner. "You have a way to blow up the quadcopter? Burning fuel ought to discourage our pursuers."

"Of course," said Argent, reaching into his belt and drawing out a dark, flat object about the size of a deck of cards. "If we put this on the fuel tank, that ought to do it."

"I suggest configuring the timer for sixty seconds," said Charles. "Indentured Worker Hammond, help me gather up some supplies."

We salvaged what equipment we could from the quadcopter. I suppose it was technically stealing, but since EcoMin agents had tried to kill me more than once today, I didn't feel that bad about it. The distant screeches of the descending aerials proved an excellent incentive to work with alacrity. Once we had gathered the equipment, Argent activated his explosive device, and we ran away from the quadcopter, back into the jungle of Arborea.

The now-familiar alien smells and sounds washed over me, the air hot and muggy. Overhead I saw several aerials circling, preparing to descend upon the quadcopter and feast. Tanner and Mr. Royale and the others hustled out of the quadcopter, rifles held ready. A crashing quadcopter ought to have scared off most of the predatory animals, but megafauna like the tankstriders might not care at all, and the tromosaurs were clever enough that the noise might only pique their curiosity.

"Keep moving!" shouted Argent, and he gestured for us to keep running.

I wondered just how powerful his little bomb was.

We sprinted further away from the damaged quadcopter, heading for the trunk of a massive tree. It was big enough that the quadcopter would have just bounced off it if we had crashed into it, so I was glad that Mulger was a better, or just a luckier, pilot than he had claimed to be. We dashed around the trunk, taking cover behind it, and I glanced back just in time to see a dozen aerials settle around the quadcopter's wreck, preparing to pry it open and feast on anything within.

Then Argent's bomb went off.

The quadcopter ripped itself apart in a spray of fire and twisted metal, and it took most of the descending aerials with it. At least a dozen of the animals blew up as burning shrapnel tore through their gas bladders, and the rest fled, screeching in indignant outrage. The fire roiled and twisted, throwing up a big plume of black smoke.

"Nice explosion," said Tanner.

"Thank you," said Argent.

"We had better move," said Tanner, adjusting the straps on his back. "The sooner we're gone, the better. Valier might send someone out to check on the explosion, and he's bound to send someone out to check on Toulon and Lysokos and their flunkies. And I don't know how much ground we have to cover to reach Outpost Town."

"Actually, I may have much-needed good news, Security Director Tanner," said Charles. "I estimate we are no more than three or four kilometers from the sonic fence around

Outpost Town. Officer Mulger covered more territory than I anticipated."

Mulger let out an indignant sound. "I did just land without killing anyone."

"Crashing," said Thompkins helpfully. "What we just survived is called crashing."

"Our successful and casualty-free crash landing will be duly noted in your commendation, Officer Mulger, should we live long enough to receive one," said Argent. "Meanwhile, Mr. Tanner is correct. We need to move. Mr. Charles, Mr. Hammond, you seem to have the most experience in this death trap, so I suggest you lead the way."

Chapter 7

Hostile Takeover

The journey went better than I expected. We only had to shoot our way through two packs of tromosaurs before we reached the relative safety of the sonic fence.

Unfortunately, that meant we had to cover the kilometer of cleared ground around Outpost Town, which meant we were exposed.

"Let's head for the landing field," said Tanner as we stood near one of the posts maintaining the sonic fence. It was a big metal cylinder that stood about three meters tall, antenna jutting out the side. It continuously put out a sound that humans couldn't hear but irritated the tromosaurs beyond all measure, keeping them away from Outpost Town. I didn't hear anything, but if I got too close to the post, my teeth started to hurt.

"Why the landing field?" said Mr. Royale.

"More cover," said Tanner, looking at Outpost Town. It was quieter than it should have been at this time of day. The large plumes of smoke rising from the administration building and one of the quadcopter hangars likely had something to do with that. "We can hide behind the ships."

"They might be guarded," said Argent. "Those special operations unit agents Valier brought with him are overrated, but we can't assume they're entirely incompetent."

"Even if they're guarded, they won't have more than four posted at the landing field," said Tanner, "And if they're over-rated, we should have no trouble shooting our way past them."

Argent frowned but said nothing. I wondered if Tanner was overeager, if in his rush to rescue Kayla we were about to make a mistake. On the other hand, I couldn't think of anything better, and he did have a point. The landing field was still full of yachts and shuttles and all the other ships belonging to the visiting guests, and all those ships provided plenty of cover.

"Whatever we do, we should do it now," said Charles. "The Safari Company typically keeps surveillance drones in the air to watch the perimeter of the forest, and unless Ecology Minister Valier specifically disabled them, they will continue their appointed rounds."

"Agreed," said Tanner. "Let's go."

We hustled past the fence and across the cleared field to the landing area. Calling it a "landing field" was a bit of an exaggeration. It was simply a large enough stretch of ground that had enough bedrock beneath it to support small starships and shuttles, so incoming ships usually landed there. Right now, the field was full to overflowing with luxury yachts and governmental shuttles. Tanner led us towards a large yacht that I thought had belonged to Alexander Toulon, and then we ducked beneath the chrome monstrosity, Tanner gesturing for silence as we did so.

A moment later the patrol drone flew overhead.

It looked a little like a smaller, snub-nosed version of the various quadcopters we had crashed today. It had a rack of cameras mounted on its belly, and I tensed as it passed, wondering if I should lift my Avenger and try to shoot it out of the sky. It was flying low enough that I might have been able to hit it.

Fortunately, Toulon's shiny chrome-dipped yacht seemed to provide adequate cover, and the drone went past without detecting us.

"Go," said Tanner. "We've got ninety seconds or so until the second drone comes around the perimeter."

We ran across the landing field, dodging past the various shuttles and yachts, and finally reached Outpost Town. Like I've said before, there are really two parts to Outpost Town. There's the shiny, fancy, expensive part with the hotels and the banquet halls and the tourist shops and whatnot. That looks expensive and sleek and inviting, kind of like Toulon's overpriced yacht. The other half of Outpost Town, the part where the men and women of Safari Company worked, was much less ostentatious. Most of the buildings were prefabricated or metal trailers, though they had held up well in the hot weather of Arborea. I saw signs of damage. Several of the equipment sheds had been blown up, and one of the hangars was still burning, throwing up one of the plumes of smoke we had seen from the edge of the jungle. Outpost Town had not fallen without a fight, though I wondered how many of the employees of Safari Company had gotten killed.

At last, we ducked into an equipment shed. It wasn't locked, but it didn't hold anything critical. Rows of cleaning drones stood in silence, powered off and waiting for maintenance. I had a brief idea of wiring them up to cause mayhem, but I discarded it.

"What now?" said Mr. Royale.

"We need more information," said Argent, "before we can decide on a move."

"Exactly," said Tanner, crossing the shed. There was a repair bench on the far wall, along with a computer terminal. "And I know just how to get that information."

"Do you think they restricted your computer access?" I said. "That's the smart thing to do."

"It is," said Tanner, typing at the keyboard, "but our friends in the Ecology Ministry have made lots of mistakes. Maybe they've made one more."

"If they assume you're dead," I said, "why shut off your computer access?"

"Exactly," said Tanner.

"Mulger, Thompkins," said Argent. "Keep an eye on the door."

The display flashed, and Tanner grinned.

"Ha!" he said. "They didn't bother to delete my account. Idiots."

"Let us continue to hope for foolish enemies," said Mr. Royale. "I imagine as security director, you have access to a lot of useful systems."

"Specifically," said Tanner, "the security cameras. Let's see what we can find here."

He accessed the security cameras and started cycling through the live feeds with practiced ease. The coverage of the security cameras wasn't great. Outpost Town had been thrown together quickly, and with a million different things that needed to be done, the security cameras had been further down the list. Nevertheless, Winston Tanner had a knack for getting his way, and most of the public areas and all of the sensitive areas of Outpost Town had cameras.

Most of which, it seemed, were still functioning.

"Hangar One," said Tanner, pointing at a flickering image. Several hundred people were in there, guarded by a squad of EcoMin's Special Ops men, guns in hand. "Looks like they rounded up most of the company personnel and put them in there."

"It makes sense," said Charles. "All our quads were out on tours." His perpetually grim expression hardened further. "It is possible we are the only survivors to make it back."

"Looks that way," said Tanner.

"Once we can call my gunship," said Argent, "we'll bring them to account."

"Wait," said Mr. Royale, pointing at the screen. "Winston, go back. Camera nineteen, I think."

Tanner frowned but obliged. Camera nineteen showed one of the big convention halls in the hotel. It was the biggest and fanciest convention hall in Outpost Town, which I knew because inevitably one of the cleaning drones broke down while attempting to vacuum the expensive carpets. Right now tables filled the hall, covered with crisp white cloth and glittering plates and silverware. Men and women sat at the tables, eating and drinking, while service drones rolled back and forth with plates of food and drink...

I blinked. "Are they... are they having a party?"

"Yep," said Tanner, his voice grim. I recognized many of the dignitaries that had descended upon the landing field earlier, attended by their bodyguards. The mood looked jovial, even celebratory.

"Wait a minute," I said. "They've been hunting people for sport all day, and now they're going to celebrate it?"

"Those who are wealthy enough to exert interplanetary influence," said Argent, "have traditionally not been unduly burdened with ethics." But there was a vicious satisfaction in his voice. "This time, we've got them red-handed sitting on top of a mountain of evidence. The Ecology Ministry and its corrupt friends are not wriggling away this time."

"Is that Valier?" I said.

Someone was giving a speech, and as I watched, I was certain that it was Valier.

"Put on the sound," said Mr. Royale.

Tanner grunted, tapped a few keys, and the voice of Paul Valier, Ecology Minister, came through the computer's speakers.

The men and women in the convention hall, Valier was saying, should congratulate themselves on their foresight and vision. Humanity already had far too great an impact on the interstellar environment, and it was time to manage and prune that impact. The Ecology Ministry had taken great strides in that direction on New Princeton, and with the project upon Arborea, an even greater step had been taken. By offering the elite live human hunts, the Ecology Ministry could prune the excess human population, preserve the environment of countless planets, rid those planets of political and social retrogressives, and turn a profit all at the same time. It was, Valier announced, the "perfect marriage of forward-thinking government and capitalist enterprise."

That was met with a round of enthusiastic applause.

Valier announced that the vehicle-based hunts had been completed and that all the renegade quadcopters had been shot down with a minimum of unavoidable casualties, which was how he glossed over the absence of Toulon and Lysokos. That erased any doubt that the rest of the company's guides and quadcopter pilots had been killed, along with any of Valier's enemies they had taken out for a tour. Tomorrow the foot-based hunts would begin, where patrons equipped with power armor could hunt the surviving Safari Company employees in designated areas outside of Outpost Town. The hunters were to be congratulated for helping to ensure a sustainable, environmentally sound future for humanity among the stars...

"Forget Most Dangerous Game," said Mr. Royale. "We've entered Masque of the Red Death territory."

"What?" said Tanner.

"Never mind," said Mr. Royale.

"Turn that nonsense off," growled Argent, glaring at the monitor. "I knew he was corrupt, but my God! He sounds as if he believes his own insanity."

"More to the point, did you hear him?" Tanner's voice sounded uncharacteristically fearful. "He said they're going to start hunting the surviving employees after the banquet! That gives us... what, an hour? Maybe two?"

"Something like that," said Tanner. He looked at Argent. "Once we call your friends on the gunship, how fast can they get there."

Argent let out a hissing breath. "Not fast enough. Three hours, if they push it."

"That is enough time for a lot of innocent people to die," said Mr. Royale.

"Then we've got to split up and do two things at once," I said. "Someone's got to go to the communications room and call the gunship, and someone's got to rescue the prisoners."

"Agreed," said Argent.

"But what are we supposed to do with the prisoners, sir?" said Mulger. "There are at least two hundred of them, and Valier has three platoons of EMSOs with him."

"They can help us fight if we get them weapons," said Tanner.

"We do that, it'll be a bloodbath," said Argent. "We might win, but the EMSOs are better armed and armored, and they'll have the bodyguards of Valier's guests to reinforce them."

"The shuttles," I said.

They all looked at me.

"Well, Valier didn't blow up our shuttles, did he?" I said, pointing in the direction of the landing field. "We could load everyone into the shuttles and have them take off. We wouldn't even have to get them into orbit. Just get everyone into the air and away from Outpost Town, and keep them out of range of the anti-air missiles until the colonel's men can land and deal with Valier's men."

Tanner, Argent, and Charles all shared a look.

"That actually might work, Spraycan," said Tanner. "Hangar One is pretty close to the landing field."

"I told you he was a smart kid," said Mr. Royale.

"There is one problem, though," said Tanner. "The shuttles don't have any guns, and a lot of those yachts are armed. Once our shuttles are in the air, how do we keep one of Valier's cronies from flying after them and shooting them down? Valier's going to realize that he's in trouble, and his first reaction will be to kill as many of the witnesses as possible."

We thought about that for a moment.

"We could turn off the sonic fence…"

"I don't see how that would help," said Tanner.

"Don't forget, the fence's parameters are configurable. We could program it to broadcast a tromosaur hunting call at maximum volume."

For the first time in the year that I had known him, Hiram Charles looked genuinely taken aback.

"That is an extremely dangerous idea, Indentured Worker Hammond," he said. "The range of the speakers upon the sonic fence extends for several miles into the jungle, and there are at least a dozen tromosaur packs moving through that area at any given moment. The hunting call will drive them into a frenzy, and they will swarm into Outpost Town heedless of any danger."

"That would make for a considerable distraction," said Argent. "It would certainly keep Valier's forces occupied."

"You're not seriously considering that," said Mr. Royale.

Tanner shrugged. "Once we've got our people in the air, we'll need to find a way to keep Valier's pals from shooting us down. If they're getting chased by a few hundred hungry tromosaurs, that will give them something else to think about."

"It'll be a slaughter," said Argent. "It would also put all of our people who don't reach the shuttles at risk."

"I know," said Tanner. He shook his head. "We'll save it as a measure of last resort. The shuttles won't have guns, but we do, and we can shoot out the airlocks and the cargo hatches if any of Valier's men try to make for the ships." He gave me a look. "That's probably safer than calling every tromosaur for twenty kilometers into Outpost Town."

I shrugged. "It's just an idea. It's not my call."

"It is agreed that our best course of action is to split up," said Charles. "I suggest one team shall have taking the communications room and contacting the Security Ministry ship as its objective. The second shall dedicate itself to liberating our fellow employees and getting them to the shuttles as quickly as possible."

"Agreed," said Argent. "I will lead Alpha Team and take the comms. I've got the codes to contact the ship, and the men aboard it will follow my orders."

"I should go with you," said Tanner, reluctantly. We all knew he wanted to find Kayla, but without the SecMin ship, all he'd likely be able to accomplish would be to die with her. "Since they haven't disabled my network access, I can probably use the consoles in the communications room."

"I will accompany you as well," said Mr. Royale. "As a member of the board, I'm supposed to have access to everything. Even if Valier or one of his lieutenants thought to lock you out, they may have overlooked me."

"I shall liberate our fellow employees and escort them to the shuttles," declared Charles. "Indentured Worker Hammond will assist me. We shall formulate a diversion or a similar stratagem."

"Mulger, Thompkins, go with them," said Argent. "If it comes to a firefight, they'll need your help."

"Sir," said Mulger.

"Let's move," said Tanner. We took a moment to synchronize our earpieces, making sure we could talk to each other, and then Tanner, Argent, and Mr. Royale headed out. I figured they would probably be all right. Tanner knew Outpost Town like the back of his hand, and Argent had survived any number of fights. I wouldn't have expected Mr. Royale to survive the jungle, but he had. I wasn't so sure about our little team's prospects.

"We need to devise a distraction," said Charles. "Something that will draw away the ministry soldiers from Hangar One."

No one had any bright ideas.

"Why does Tanner always call you Spraycan?" said Mulger.

"I kind of defaced an official portrait of Paul Valier. That's how I ended up here."

Thompkins guffawed.

"Seems a little harsh," said Mulger. "Sending you to this death trap of a planet for petty vandalism. Why not just have you clean off the portrait?"

I blinked. Something in Mulger's words made me think of something.

"Hey," I said. "I think I just had an idea."

"I hope it is a good one," said Mulger. "There are at least six EMSO men guarding the prisoners. I don't want to have to fight them all myself."

"Mind if I have a look?" I said, gesturing at the computer.

Thompkins grunted and stepped to the side. I started typing, Charles looking over my shoulder. I didn't actually know how to use the security cameras, but I had seen Tanner do it enough times, and the system wasn't that complicated.

After a moment, I found what I wanted, and I grinned.

"There," I said, pointing at the screen. "Right there."

"It's a prefab building near Hangar One," said Mulger. "Looks like a barracks."

"It is a low-cost motel for the crews of visiting ships," said Charles. "The Safari Company uses it to provide low-cost, short-term accommodations for them. I fail to see how this is useful to our present difficulties, Indentured Worker Hammond."

"It is useful," I said, "because I spent a lot of time fixing those stupid cleaning drones, and the drones are stored at the motel. Which is currently unguarded."

Charles blinked at me, and then he nodded in approval.

It didn't take long to raid the motel and load up on the equipment that we needed. The motel was unguarded, though it faced Hangar One, and everyone inside the hangar would be able to see the front doors of the motel without any difficulty. Fortunately, we circled around to the back and entered through the service entrance by the kitchen and the laundry rooms.

That was just as well because the kitchen and the laundry rooms held what I needed.

"What are those things?" said Mulger, blinking.

Row after row of industrial-grade cleaning drones filled the kitchen and the laundry rooms, silent and motionless. They looked like heavy cylinders squatting upon wheeled treads, each one standing about four feet tall. Various manipulator arms and sprayers jutted from the cylinders, and a row of chemical tanks encircled the base of the cylinders, holding the various cleaners and solvents the drones used in their tasks.

"Cleaning drones," I said.

Thompkins grunted. "Robot janitors, basically."

"Yes," I said.

"What are they doing here?" said Mulger.

"Well," I said, squeezing through one of the laundry rooms to a supply cabinet, "they were all defective. Or they were sabotaged. Tanner and Mr. Royale thought a faction inside EcoMin wanted the company to fail, so we had all sorts of equipment troubles and mechanical breakdowns." I paused as a thought struck me. "Though considering how Valier's gone nuts and was planning to hunt people for sport, it makes sense that some of his underlings would oppose his plans. Suppose I should take back all the mean things I said about them."

"Don't do anything rash," said Mulger in a dry voice. "So what do we need these things for?"

"That was my last major project before Valier showed up for the grand opening," I said. I rooted around in the cabinet for a moment, scowling, and then I found where I had put it. I drew out a computer tablet, a big, thick, clunky ruggedized device designed to operate in HVAC rooms and other dirty, grimy places. "I had to fix all fifty of these stupid things, so I still have root access for their operating systems."

"Which means you can make them do whatever you want," said Mulger, comprehension dawning on his face.

"Yeah," I said. "Tanner said he wanted a distraction, so here it is."

"I think we can use that," said Mulger. "Where did you learn to fix cleaning drones?"

I shrugged. "They are a lot less complicated than my Uncle Morgan's autonomous tractors."

Mulger, Thompkins, and Charles launched into a brief tactical discussion while I unlocked the tablet and started entering commands. Fortunately, the tablet's operating system included a wildcard function so I could control all fifty of the cleaning drones at once, rather than activating them each one individually, and soon the laundry room was filled with the dull whine of the drones' motors firing up.

"Ready?" said Mulger once he and Charles had decided upon a plan.

"I think so," I said, squinting at the tablet. "Let's see…"

I tapped in a command, and suddenly, every single one of the cleaning drones came to life, turning right and lifting their scrubbing arms.

All of them could talk using a synthetic speech engine, and they had voice recognition that permitted them to respond to voice commands. In addition to the synthetic speech, they also had a bunch of preprogrammed responses recorded by some big-name actress back on New Princeton.

"Good morning!" said all fifty of the cleaning drones in cheery unison. "I am looking forward to helping you lead a cleaner, happier life this morning! How can we achieve greater well-being today?"

Thompkins swore. "They sound like my ex-wife. An army of them."

I suddenly had a vision of fifty drones speaking in the voice of Theresa Graff, and I shuddered. It was just as well that we had broken up after she had gotten me arrested.

"Let's move," said Mulger, taking the safety off his Avenger.

I sent another command to my little drone army, and they turned on their treads and started making their way to the motel's lobby. Mulger, Thompkins, Charles and I headed for the stairs as the drones rolled past us.

Static crackled in my earpiece, followed by Tanner's voice. "Charles? How are you doing?"

"The plan proceeds," said Charles, tapping his ear. "Indentured Worker Hammond has taken control of the cleaning drones, and we are moving into position. You?"

"We're in the administrative building, moving through the service hallways," said Tanner. "The place is moderately guarded, but they're not on alert. It looks like most of Valier's men are in the security center and the convention hall, but there are only two guarding the communication room. I think we should coordinate our attacks. Soon as we move, they'll start calling for help, and the more confusion we can sow about where we're hitting them, the better."

"Agreed," said Charles. "There are pilots among the prisoners, and that will expedite getting them to safety aboard the shuttles."

"Kayla's rated on one of the shuttles," said Tanner as we walked into the motel's second-floor lounge. He spoke as if he was utterly certain that she was still alive. Maybe that was how he had kept himself going through the whole disaster. "She can fly one of them."

"Good enough," said Mulger.

Argent's voice came into the conversation. "Listen. Do not hesitate to shoot to kill any of the EMSOs, or any of the armed bodyguards. Everything we will do here today is quite clearly a matter of self-defense and I have already recorded an official statement to that effect."

In other words, we had a literal license to kill. But it didn't make me feel dangerous. It made me feel scared enough to wet myself. "What about the guests?" I said.

"It's your call," said Argent. "When in doubt, take them out."

Charles, Mulger, and Thompkins set up in the lounge, cracking the windows open and taking position. From up here we had an excellent view of the doors of Hangar One, including the hundreds of prisoners secured there. I spotted eight EMSOs standing guard, but none of them saw us. There were only eight of them, and with over three hundred prisoners to watch, their attention was on the prisoners. Which made sense, as a mass rush of the prisoners might overwhelm them. On the other hand, the guards had military-grade automatic weapons, so they could mow down a lot of prisoners before they were overrun.

"Indentured Worker Hammond," said Charles. "Status of drones?"

"Getting there," I said, keying the EMSO soldiers and their locations into the tablet. It really wasn't that different than programming Uncle Morgan's autonomous tractors. The drones could be set to clean different locations, so I configured the empty space outside Hangar One as a banquet hall, and the individual soldiers as tables in that banquet hall.

"Gentlemen, select your shots," said Mulger, kneeling by the window and taking aim. "I have the leftmost pair."

The others confirmed their choices. The eight soldiers stood there, little realizing they had all been marked for death.

I scrolled through the options on the tablet. Once the location had been configured, you could also program the drones to the specific kind of cleaning needed. The drones would use a different set of tools and solvents on, say, a banquet hall table than on a carpeted hallway.

For the soldiers, I selecting the cleaning profile best suited for cleaning a soiled hotel bed soaked in the bodily fluids of a drug-addled rock star with impulse control issues. This profile came with various warnings about toxins and improper ingestion, accompanied by a long list of all the terrible, horrible, very bad things that would happen to anyone who happened to inhale the industrial-grade cleaning solution.

Fortunately, I had root access, so it was easy to override those warnings.

"We are in position and ready," said Mulger. "Hammond?"

"Ready," I said, resting my finger on the EXECUTE button.

"All right," said Tanner. "Good luck, gentlemen. We go in three... two... one... now!"

I tapped the EXECUTE button as I heard the sound of gunfire erupt in my earpiece.

The lobby doors swung open, and fifty cleaning drones exited the building and rolled out towards the EMSO soldiers, wobbling a little as their treads gripped the asphalt. That got the soldiers' attention, and they turned towards the motel, leveling their guns at the drones. Once they saw that the newcomers were in fact harmless cleaning drones, they lowered their weapons, and two or three of them laughed.

Then all the drones started speaking in unison.

"Good afternoon!" they announced, rolling towards the soldiers. "At Outpost Town, Safari Company wishes all our guests to have an enjoyable and pleasant stay. We are delighted to maintain clean facilities for all our guests, and will now be cleaning your rooms. Gratuities are not required."

The drones divided themselves into eight groups, each group heading for one of the soldiers.

"Hammond," said Mulger. "Are any of those cleaners and solvents flammable?"

"Probably," I said. "I don't actually know."

"Guess we're about to find out," said Mulger.

The eight groups of drones rolled towards their soldiers, and right about then I think the EMSO guys realized that something was up.

"Hey!" shouted one of the EMSO soldiers, backing away from the approaching drone. "Go away, get back!"

"Cleaning," chorused the drones, "will now commence."

In perfect unison, all fifty drones sprayed the EMSO men with foaming cleaner.

We were thirty yards away and one floor up, with closed windows between us and the drones, but even through all that, the odor of the chemicals made my nose tingle and my eyes water. The soldiers were wearing combat suits, and their masks must have filtered out the worst of it, but some of the smell must have gotten through, and the foam covered the faceplates of their masks anyway.

They started shooting at the drones, which masked the initial shots taken by Mulger, Thompkins, and Charles. They had taken down four before the EMSOs even realized we were there. One of them got off a shot that shattered a window, and Charles responded by shooting him in the chest. We ducked and took cover as the surviving EMSOs started shooting at the motel, their powerful weapons chewing through the windows, but they found out that it's really hard to shoot straight when your visor is covered with cleaning foam and your respirator is jammed with extremely poisonous fumes. Charles popped up five times and fired single shots, and with the last shot, the sound of all resistance stopped.

"All targets down," announced Mulger. "Repeat, all targets down."

I waited for a response from Tanner and Argent and Mr. Royale but didn't hear anything. Guess they were busy. The cleaning drones busied themselves by cleaning the downed EMSO soldiers. They might be dead, but the drones would make sure they left sparkling clean corpses behind for the funeral.

"Let us proceed to Hangar One and direct Technical Writer Tanner and the other survivors to the shuttles," said Charles.

"Who?" said Mulger, straightening up as Thompkins checked his gun.

"Kayla, Tanner's wife," I said, sending a command to the tablet. The drones stopped spraying cleaning solvent over the dead men. "She can fly one."

We hurried downstairs and exited through the lobby, jogging towards Hangar One.

The chemical smell was overpowering. We were in the open air, and the smell of cleaners was nearly overpowering. In an enclosed space, it would have killed you in your tracks. The chemical reek probably killed all the bacteria on my skin, which was just as well, because I didn't smell so great after all our adventures in the jungle.

I was pleased, but not surprised, to see that Director Hoskins and Kayla had taken charge of the prisoners. Kayla had already helped herself to one of the dead soldiers' guns, as had Hoskins, and the rest of the prisoners were starting to stream out of the hangar. Charles and I took the lead, walking in front of Mulger and Thompkins, since Kayla and Hoskins and the others would not recognize them.

"Sam? Hiram?" said Kayla, looking from me to Charles. "Did you do this?"

"Yes, ma'am," I said. "We should probably hurry." I jerked a thumb at Mulger and Thompkins. "These guys are here from the Security Ministry. Their colonel is with your husband, and they're breaking into the communications room to call to a SecMin gunship in the outer system. Once they do, the ship will come, arrest Valier and everyone else, and we'll get everyone to safety."

"What about all of us?" said Hoskins, sweating profusely in the muggy heat of Arborea. "Where should we go?"

"The shuttles," said Charles. "Security Director Tanner suggested that we take the employees aboard the shuttles and get them into the air. That way they will be safe from any crossfire between Colonel Argent's men and Ecology Minister Valier's soldiers."

"That's a good plan," said Hoskins. "Kayla, can you fly one of the shuttles?"

"Yeah," she said looking at me. "Fisher and Ramirez are rated on the shuttles too. Between the three of us, we can get everyone into the air. The sooner we go, the better." The skin around her eyes tightened. "Those EMSO guys shot fifteen of us getting us rounded up in Hangar One. They said they were going to release us into the jungle and let the guests hunt us for sport."

Behind her, the employees were streaming out of the hangar and were directed towards the landing field as Hoskins shouted instructions.

I nodded. "This whole thing is Valier's idea. I think Alexander Toulon paid a couple million credits for the privilege of shooting down our quadcopter."

"What happened?" said Kayla.

"Mrs. Tanner," said Hoskins, "we had better move now. If there is going to be shooting, most of our people don't have weapons and will be sitting ducks. The sooner we are in the air and out of missile range, the better."

"Yes, right," said Kayla, shaking her head. I could almost see her pulling herself together. "Sam, when you see Winston, tell him…"

"Hey," I said. "No time for that. Whatever you have to say to him, you can tell him yourself once this is all over."

Kayla smiled. "Thank you, Sam. Good luck."

She turned and followed Hoskins, helping to herd the employees along to the landing field and the waiting shuttles.

An idea came to me, and I jogged after Hoskins. "Wait!"

He turned and blinked back at me. "What is it?"

"Before you go, I need access to the control for the sonic fence," I said.

He frowned, sweat trickling down his jaw. "Why? Aren't you coming with us?"

"No," I said. "If this goes bad, you'll need a distraction to escape, and changing the frequencies on the fence will make for a pretty big distraction."

His frowned deepened, and then I saw him get it. He started to speak, thought better of it, then took my tablet and entered a few commands.

"Only use this if you have to," said Hoskins, handing it back to me. "And only once we've got the shuttles in the air. Understand?"

"Yes, sir," I said.

He offered a tight smile. "Well, Valier wanted a hunt. We'll see how he likes being on the other end of one."

He turned and hurried to join the others, and I returned to Mulger, Charles, and Thompkins.

"We're going to go help the colonel, I assume?" said Thompkins.

"That's right," said Mulger. He looked at Charles and me. "We haven't heard from him and the others since the shooting started." He was right, come to think of it. I had been so focused on our own situation and getting our people moving towards the shuttles that I hadn't realized it. "I hope that doesn't mean…"

My earpiece crackled, and Tanner's voice came into my ears.

"Charles? Spraycan?" said Tanner. "You there?"

"Yeah," I said. His voice sounded strained. "We're good. We took out the EMSO guys and got the employees on the way to the field. Kayla's okay, and so is Director Hoskins. They're getting the survivors to the shuttles."

"Good," said Tanner. "Here's the problem. We need help. We're pinned down outside the communications room."

"Wait," said Mulger. "Did you contact the ship?"

"Negative. Our objective has not been completed," said Argent, his voice tight. There was a burst of static in the background. No, not static, gunfire. "I repeat, our objective has not been completed. We have not been able to summon reinforcements."

I swallowed. Our whole plan was based on calling Argent's gunship down on Valier and his men. If we didn't get reinforcements here in time, Valier could shoot down the shuttles. Heck, he didn't even need a functioning ship to do it. He could send out his quadcopters out after them and shoot them down.

And once Valier realized that people were escaping his twisted hunt, he would realize he couldn't leave any witnesses alive, which meant he would have to kill us all.

"How many are there?" said Charles.

"At least ten, they're in two groups and they've got us in a crossfire." Tanner's voice was drowned out by a series of rapid gunshots. "Make that nine; the colonel just nailed one."

"Hang on Tanner," I said. "We're on our way."

"Which way?" said Mulger.

"This way," said Charles, pointing towards Outpost Town. "If we cut through the primary HVAC building, we can enter the administration building through the service corridors and flank them."

"Lead on," said Mulger.

Charles jogged towards the HVAC building, Mulger and Thompkins following him. I hesitated, tapped a command on the tablet I still held in one hand, and then ran after them.

A moment later, the survivors of my drone army turned and rolled after me.

Chapter 8
Tactics For Beginners

No one saw us as we hurried across Safari Town and made our way into the HVAC building. Charles didn't have access to the HVAC building, but my maintenance codes were good throughout the town, so I unlocked one of the side doors.

"I wonder why Valier didn't send anyone here," I said.

"I think," said Mulger, opening the door and peering around. The sound of laboring air handlers came to my ears. "I think this is a one-time deal."

"What do you mean?" I said.

"He's been so sloppy," said Mulger, sweeping his Avenger back and forth as he checked for hostiles. "EcoMin can't possibly be planning a permanent facility here. Without constant maintenance, Outpost would fall apart in a week."

He had no idea how right he was.

I tapped a command on the tablet, telling the drones to enter through the service doors of the administrative building and take up position in the corridors outside the communications room.

Mulger beckoned, and we stepped through the door. The HVAC building provided air and heat for the entire town and consequently was the size of a small sports stadium. Of course, machinery filled most of the space, and the hums and rattles and groans of stressed metal filled my ears, accompanied by the constant whine of the fans and the vibrations in the floor.

"So you think he plans to kill everyone and let Outpost Town rot?" I said.

"Yeah," said Mulger. Charles pointed, and we hastened down a narrow corridor between two massive machines. "He probably made ten billion credits or so off this. Keeping a permanent facility here would be like leaving out a big box with the words INCRIMINATING EVIDENCE on the lid in bright red letters. So he kills everybody, collects his money, and leaves. Then EcoMin announces that some sort of disaster happened to Safari Company, and the tromosaurs ate everyone, declares the entire planet an off-limits Red Zone, and the evidence is buried for his lifetime and beyond."

"Evil, most evil, and yet inspired," said Charles, almost admiringly.

I gave a dismayed shake of my head. It made a horrible amount of sense. Maybe Valier had known all along that people within the Ministry had been attempting to sabotage his plans, and maybe he hadn't cared. After all, if he was going to kill everyone and abandon Arborea, what did a few equipment failures matter in the end? All that he cared about was ensuring that all the evidence of his atrocities was completely hidden.

Well, that wasn't going to happen. He would have to kill all of us first, and we weren't going down without a fight.

"No more talking," said Mulger as we reached the other end of the HVAC room. "The noise from the machines will have drowned out our voices, but I don't know how far any noise will carry in the administrative building."

"Pretty far, actually," I said.

"Right," said Thompkins. "So, shut up unless it's mission-critical."

"Ready?" whispered Mulger.

I nodded. Then I locked the tablet's screen and hooked it to my belt. I shifted my Avenger to my left hand and used my right to enter the access code on the door. It beeped and released, and I stepped back. Charles opened the door, and the two SecMin soldiers leveled their weapons, pointing them at the corridor beyond the door.

It was empty. The lights were on, but the corridor was deserted. The doors on either side of the corridor opened into large rooms lined with cubicles, where the workers responsible for the day-to-day paperwork of Safari Company toiled at their computer terminals. Mulger and Thompkins moved forward in a brisk, efficient, military manner, clearing both of the office rooms.

"Clear," said Mulger.

"Tanner?" I said, tapping my earpiece. "We're in the admin building. Where are you?"

"Employee lounge across the hall from the communications room," said Tanner. More static crackled over the earpiece as someone shot at him, and I heard Argent swearing in the background. "The EMSOs are at either end of the hallway now, and they've got us caught in a crossfire. If we try to step out of the lounge, we're dead. The walls are thick enough to stop their bullets, but if they bring up any heavier weapons or find some grenades, they can blow the lounge and take us."

"Roger," said Mulger. He looked at us. "Suggestions?"

I shared a glance with Charles.

"The communications room is on the ground floor by the network rooms," said Charles. "If we cut through the office wing, through server room number three, I think we can take the southern group off guard."

"What about the northern group?" said Mulger.

"I think I might be able to distract them," I said, pulling the thick tablet from my belt and unlocking.

"What?" said Tanner. "How?"

Thompkins snorted. "Sam Hammond, drone commander."

"What did he say?" said Tanner.

"You heard him," I said, tapping in some commands. "I brought my drone army."

"All right," said Tanner. "Make it fast. They're calling for reinforcements. If they get here, we're finished. Get a move on!"

"You heard the man," said Mulger. "Let's go. Charles?"

"This way," said Charles. "I shall take point. I may need Indentured Worker Hammond to unlock a few doors along the way."

We hurried through the maze of corridors in the administration building. I had spent so much time here repairing things or doing banal tasks like filling out forms that it felt seriously strange to run around in hunting armor and toting an Avenger rifle. Charles led us through a wing of offices and conference rooms and across the main lobby. The lobby was the biggest room in the building, and for a hastily-constructed prefab, it looked pretty nice, with a fake marble floor, a big fancy desk of fake wood for the receptionist, and massive doors of reinforced, transparent metal that could stop anything short of a tankstrider from getting in.

Right about then, our luck ran out.

Four EMSOs came through the massive doors just as we entered the lobby, and they saw us before we saw them, thanks to the position of the lighting in the ceiling. Charles shouted a warning, and we dove for cover just in time. Mulger, Thompkins, and Charles ducked back into the corridor, firing to keep the EMSOs at bay. I couldn't make it back in time, so I sprinted for the receptionist's desk, vaulted over it, and landed on the floor. I suppose it looked really cool, but landing on the hard floor hurt, and nearly knocked the breath out of me. Still, it hurt less than getting shot would have, and the desk kept the soldiers' shots from hitting me.

I crawled to the edge of the desk and squeezed off a few shots to no effect. The EMSO soldiers were using the half-opened transparent doors as cover, and our Avengers didn't have the kind of firepower we needed to punch through the doors. Worse, I saw one of the EMSO men wrestling with a long black tube. He had a rocket launcher, similar to the one Toulon had used to bring down our quadcopter in the jungle. One shot from that thing would kill Charles, Mulger, and Thompkins.

Or it would blast the receptionist's desk to dust and kill me in the process.

Then we got lucky.

I saw a flicker of light through the doors, and I saw a way out.

The surviving cleaning drones had arrived. I belatedly realized that I hadn't given them permission to use the service entrances. Their programming had taken over, and they had wheeled themselves to the front doors of the administrative building to wait for further instructions. I grabbed the tablet from my belt and entered a command just as the first of the drones rolled into the lobby.

The drones stopped, turned, and started cleaning the EMSO soldiers. I don't think the soldiers realized the threat until it was too late. The drones started spraying them with arcs of white foam, obscuring their vision. They turned in confusion, and started at the drones.

That was the wrong thing to do. Charles promptly shot two of them, and Mulger and Thompkins accounted for the other two. I tapped the tablet again, telling the drones to stop cleaning, and they complied, accompanied by a chorus of announcements that they were glad to serve and ensure a pleasant experience for guests.

"Anyone hit?" said Mulger, stepping out of the corridor.

"No," I said, getting to my feet.

"I applaud your excellent timing, Indentured Worker Hammond," said Charles. "Our tactical position was untenable."

"I just got lucky," I said. "I told the drones to come to the administrative building. I forgot to tell them to come through the service entrance. So they showed up here."

"Lucky for us," said Mulger as Charles jogged over to the dead EMSO soldiers. I wondered if he had decided to loot the bodies. "We're going to hit the southern group keeping the colonel and your friends pinned down. Can you send the drones to hit the northern one?"

"Hold on," I said, trying to remember the layout of the administrative building. "Yeah, I think I can. The corridor outside the communications room runs north to south. If Charles takes us through server room three, we'll come out on the south end of the corridor." I pulled up a map on the tablet. "Yeah. I can send the drones to circle around." I started tapping commands into the device. "I'll tell them the entire corridor there is a biohazard and to clean it at maximum possible strength."

"Good man," said Mulger. "Charles?"

Charles jogged back towards us, his Avenger slung on his harness, something thick and black and heavy-looking in his arms.

"A rocket launcher?" I said.

"It may prove useful," said Charles. "One never knows."

I couldn't argue with that. I finished entering the commands for the drones, and the tablet beeped at me. The drones began whirring towards one of the corridors leading off towards the server rooms and network closets.

"Watch it, Charles," said Mulger. "We're in a closed space. Don't blow us up."

"Certainly not," said Charles. "This way."

We headed down a hallway, took a right, and I opened the door to server room three. It was a big room, though not as large as the HVAC room, and filled with racks of humming servers, thousands of blinking green and blue and red LEDs flashing in the dim light. It was very cold, and the air was the driest I had ever encountered on Arborea. Maybe if I had gone into system administration instead of KwikBreet machine repair, I wouldn't have found myself in so much danger.

We reached the other end of the server room, and Charles held up a hand to halt before the door.

"As soon as we go around this corner, I think we will be right behind the southern group of EMSO soldiers."

"Hit them hard and hit them fast," said Thompkins.

"Hammond, are your drones in position?" said Mulger.

"Let me check," I said, bringing up the appropriate display on the tablet. It had never occurred to me that I could fight an enemy using a tablet and an army of janitorial drones, but I suppose you really do learn something new every day. "Looks like... nine of them are close enough. If I send them around the corner, they'll go into full biohazard mode and start scrubbing down the soldiers."

Thompkins grunted. "Think that'll distract them long enough for us to take out the southern group?"

"I don't know," I said. "Probably not. The drones are loud when they're working, but gunshots are louder. We'll get a couple of seconds, maybe."

"Fortunately," said Charles, patting his rocket launcher, "a solution is at hand."

"Seriously?" I said. "You're going to set that thing off in here?"

Charles shrugged. "I will not be firing it in the server room, Indentured Worker Hammond. I suppose I might accidentally destroy the nearby conference room as collateral damage."

"Good enough," said Mulger. "Colonel?" He tapped his earpiece.

Argent's voice hissed in my ear. "Where are you? You'd better hurry up! I think they're waiting for reinforcements with grenades."

I looked at Charles's rocket launcher. "Yeah, about that. We sort of ran into the reinforcements and took their rocket launcher. You should probably take cover."

There was a momentary pause.

"Roger," said Argent at last. "Bring the noise."

"Ready?" said Mulger.

"Yeah," I said, resting my finger on the EXECUTE button. "Just say the world."

Mulger nodded. "On three. One, two... three!"

Thompkins pulled the door open, and I tapped the EXECUTE button, sending the command to the waiting drones. At the same instant, Mulger and Thompkins surged through the door, Charles following them with his newly acquired rocket launcher. As fast as I could, I clipped the tablet to my belt, grabbed my Avenger again and followed the others through the door.

I swung around the corner and into a firefight.

It was going our way. Five EMSO soldiers blocked the corridor ahead of us, and Mulger and Thompkins had already shot three of them in the back. I shot another one, and the final EMSO leaped at us, using his gun as a club. Mulger dodged, and Thompkins dropped the man with three quick rounds. At the far end of the corridor, I saw another group of EMSO soldiers aiming at us, but then I heard the sound of the cleaning drones, and the soldiers suddenly disappeared in a torrent of white foam.

With perfect calm, Charles dropped to one knee, braced the rocket launcher against his shoulder, and squeezed the trigger.

That was when I learned there were a couple of problems with firing a rocket launcher in an enclosed space like the corridor of an office building.

First, there was the smoke. The rocket howled out of the launcher and left a plume of white smoke in its wake, immediately obscuring our vision. The second problem was the heat from the discharge, as flame spraying out of the tail of the rocket set the walls on fire. The third problem was the recoil. I don't think Charles was prepared for the force of the recoil, and it knocked him back sprawling onto the floor.

Fortunately, none of those problems mattered when the warhead struck the far wall.

The northern end of the corridor ripped apart in a fireball, the administrative building shaking around us. I threw myself to the floor, and Mulger and Thompkins followed suit, while Charles was already there. Something clicked in the ceiling overhead, and the fire suppressant systems kicked in, foam spraying out over the walls and floor. I lifted my head as the fireball winked out, swinging my Avenger towards the northern end of the corridor.

The EMSO men were no longer a problem. The rocket had made enough of a mess that identifying the bodies would probably prove difficult. The explosion had wiped out a bunch of my drones too, but reinforcements were rolling in, their fire suppressant programming taking over as they sprayed the walls and floor with flame retardant.

"Huh," I said, getting to my feet. My voice sounded a little shaky in my ears. "Guess that hallway's going to really be a biohazard after all."

"That backblast was worse than I expected," said Charles as Thompkins helped him up.

Mulger just shook his head.

A door on the left hissed open, and I saw the business end of an Avenger poke out, followed by Tanner's head. He looked at the wreckage in the corridor, at me, at the wreckage again, and then back to me.

"What did you do?" he said.

"Rocket launcher," I said. "I think they were planning to use it on you."

"Morons," said Colonel Argent, following Tanner into the corridor. "If they fired that into the lounge door, they would have caught themselves in the shrapnel. The corridor is too narrow."

"I think we are agreed," said Mr. Royale, "that the EcoMin operators have not been paragons of competence."

"I don't think Valier cares about damaging the buildings," I said. "Mulger had an idea, and I think he's right. He thinks Valier never intended for Outpost Town to be a permanent installation. He'll make a few billion credits, kill us all, wreck the facility, announce there was another natural disaster, and walk away clean."

Tanner and Mr. Royale shared a look.

"That makes a disturbing amount of sense," said Mr. Royale.

"It's exactly his style, too," said Tanner. "Do a lot of damage and wreck a lot of lives, and then slither off someplace with a lot of money. Kayla can tell you all about that. It's the same thing on a grander scale."

"Undoubtedly," said Mr. Royale. "Then let's make sure Minister Valier gets caught with his hand in the till. Colonel?"

"Any guards in there?" Mulger asked, pointing to the door on the right side of the corridor.

"No, we had just tried the door when the two of them came around the corner. We got one, but the other one drove us back into the conference room, then called for help."

At Argent's nod, Tanner unlocked the door, and we slogged through ankle-deep fire suppressant foam into the communications room. It was smaller than the server room but big enough that we could all fit inside without crowding. Consoles lined the walls, and a central computer station with three monitors sat in the center of the room. The computers in this room controlled all the phone and radio transmissions in Outpost Town and handled calls from any outbound quadcopters. The computers also controlled any outgoing transmissions to space vessels, which meant we could call Argent's men in their gunship.

Or so I hoped.

Tanner unlocked one of the consoles, and Argent at once sat down, plugged in a headset, and started typing. I leaned against one of the consoles, keeping an eye on the door, and a wave of weariness went through me. It had been a long and unpleasant day, and it wasn't over yet. I really wanted to lie down and close my eyes, but that would be a bad idea.

"Acknowledged," said Argent, and he straightened up with a satisfied look on his face. "Gentlemen, support is now on the way. *Mathey* is heading at full speed for near orbit. ETA is in a little over three hours."

The tablet at my belt started vibrating. I frowned, propped my Avenger against the console, and lifted the device.

"Excellent," said Mr. Royale. "What now?"

"The shuttles are in the air," said Tanner. "All three of them. We had better go to the landing field and disable as many of the other ships as we can manage. Then we'll take Ian's ship and get into the air until the *Mathey* arrives to shut down Valier."

I scrolled through the displays on the tablet. One by one, the tablet was losing its connection to the cleaning drones. Frowning, I checked the status for each of the drones. I could still control the ones that had made it into the administrative building. I couldn't control any of the ones that hadn't figured out how to get into the building yet.

I had lost contact with them.

Or, more likely, they had been destroyed.

"Tanner," I said. "Can you get to the cameras from here?"

"Yeah," he said, frowning. "What is it?"

"I think we had better have a look outside," I said. "Right now."

Tanner only nodded, dropped into another seat, and access the security cameras. The computer's display went from a listing of transmission logs to the blue-tinted images from the security cameras.

The first thing I saw was a group of about thirty EMSOs heading down the street towards the administrative building we were in, combat rifles and rocket launchers in hand as they strode over the wreckage of my cleaning drones.

"Colonel, we have a problem," I said.

Chapter 9

Man Against Nature

"We had better withdraw," said Argent. "We can't take on two platoons."

"Fortunately," said Tanner, "I'm still the Security Director of Safari." He entered a sequence of commands into the console. The computer beeped and asked him for a voiceprint, and Tanner recited his full name, followed by an identification code. Again the computer beeped, and Tanner put his right palm on the screen. The display flashed once more.

Then I heard a humming noise, followed by distant clanging.

"Lockdown," said Tanner. "I've sealed off all the doors and windows. Valier and his men aren't getting in here."

"We're not getting out either," said Argent.

"We were not getting out anyway," said Charles. "Look, Colonel Argent."

Charles reached over and adjusted the camera display, and it shifted to show the sides of the administrative building. The EMSOs had moved to cover all the entrances, and I saw that the various bands of bodyguards had joined as well.

The administrative building was surrounded, and we were stuck inside it.

"We're trapped," said Mr. Royale.

"Think we can shoot our way out?" said Tanner.

"Not likely," said Argent, pointing at the screen. "Look at how they're setting up kill zones in all four directions. If we try to go through them, they'll take us all out before we can reach cover."

"They won't even need to bother with that," said Thompkins. "If they take one of the ships on the landing field, they can crash it into the administrative building and kill us all."

"Would one of the guests let Valier use their ship for ramming the building?" I said.

Argent shrugged. "Toulon and Lysokos aren't using theirs anymore, are they?"

I hated to admit it, but that was a good point.

I heard a sudden beeping in my earpiece.

"He's calling us," said Tanner. "Let's hear what he has to say."

He tapped his earpiece and entered a few commands on one of the consoles.

A moment later Valier's smooth politician's voice came out of the speakers in the console.

"This is the Minister of Ecology, Paul Valier," he said, as calm and poised as if he was strolling along the streets of Wilson City back on New Princeton. "I am addressing the terrorists who presently occupy the administration center. Your illegal and unauthorized insurrection has been contained, and the security forces of the ministry have you surrounded. I suggest you surrender at once in order to avoid any further unnecessary loss of life. If you do not come out within ten minutes, the building will be destroyed, and all the three of the shuttles that recently took off from the landing field will be shot down. I repeat, you have ten minutes to comply and exit the building."

Tanner swore once, slapped the console with his palm, and stepped back.

"I hate to say it," said Mulger, "but maybe we should surrender. The ship is on its way. If he doesn't shoot everyone right away, Captain Butler can free the survivors."

Tanner shook his head. "I don't think there will be any survivors. If we surrender, Valier will just kill us out of hand. There's too much at stake for him to let us live. This scheme of his only works if he doesn't leave any witnesses behind, and we've all seen far too much."

"Perhaps we can stall him," said Charles. "If we delay long enough, the ship will arrive."

"I doubt we can stall for three hours," said Tanner. He rubbed his broad forehead. "We should call Kayla and Hoskins first, have them take the shuttles into space. They should be able to get into orbit before the deadline."

Valier repeated his message once more, his smooth voice filling the communications room.

"I have an idea," I said in a quiet voice.

"Oh, you do, Spraycan?" snapped Tanner. "Why don't..." He stopped himself. "No. I'm not thinking clearly. You've handled yourself well all day. All right, Sam. What's your idea?"

I don't think he had ever called me by my actual name before.

"Before he got on the shuttle," I said, lifting my tablet, "Hoskins gave me access to the sonic fence. I can reconfigure it to emit a hunting call for the tromosaurs."

They stared at me in silence.

"You realize that would call every tromosaur pack within fifteen kilometers into town," said Charles.

"Yeah," I said. "That's the point. See, Valier and all his goons and everyone else are outside. They're gathered around us here. They won't be anywhere near the fence so they won't realize what is happening until it's too late. The tromosaurs won't be able to get in here. We can force Valier to surrender, tell him to lay down his guns in exchange for coming in here."

Again we looked at each other in silence.

"I can't think of anything better," said Mr. Royale.

"Well," said Argent, "if we're going to die, I suppose it doesn't matter if we're going to be shot or if we're going to be eaten by tromosaurs."

"I would highly recommend being shot, Colonel," Charles told him. Argent only raised an eyebrow.

"Do it," said Tanner. "Do it now. I'll call Valier back and tell him we're willing to negotiate a surrender. If we're lucky, we can keep him talking until it's too late for him to do anything about the lizards."

I nodded and tapped the command into my tablet. The machine took a moment to communicate with the computers controlling the sonic fence and then it beeped an acknowledgment. The waveform parameter and volume level had been changed.

That meant the fence was now telling any tromosaur within range that wounded, defenseless prey was within. If those ill-fated biologists of the past expedition were correct about tromosaur hunting cries, that should drive the creatures into a total frenzy.

"Valier," said Tanner. "This is Security Director Winston Tanner of Safari Company. I would like to request a meeting to discuss terms and conditions for surrender."

There was a pause.

"Splendid," said Valier. "I am pleased that you are able to see reason. My terms are this. You will lay down your weapons, exit the building immediately, and put yourselves into the custody of my security forces."

Tanner snorted. "You know, for a politician, I think you'd be better at negotiating."

"I am an excellent negotiator," said Valier. "You see, the ability to make demands in a negotiation is predicated upon one's position of strength. You don't have any strength in this negotiation."

"That's strange," said Tanner, "because I seem to see a lot of guns and bombs nearby."

"Which would serve you well if this were a simple firefight," said Valier. "It is not. I need only crash one of the ships into the administrative building to rid myself of you. Perhaps you were the reason poor Alexander Toulon didn't make it back to Outpost Town? Well, he was always a reckless one. I'm sure it would amuse him to know that his overpriced chrome-plated yacht avenged his death."

"I'm afraid you're misinformed," said Tanner. "We also have our own strengths in this negotiation."

"Oh?" said Valier. "This ought to be amusing. Do explain, Mr. Tanner."

"The various bombs," said Tanner, "that we have hidden around Outpost Town will be going off soon. Perhaps you would like to know where they are in exchange for letting us go."

Valier scoffed. "Come now, Mr. Tanner. The destruction of Outpost Town would, in fact, make the rest of my day easier. That is not much a threat."

"Depends on where the bombs are," said Tanner. He grinned. "Have you looked at where you are standing, Minister Valier? You might want to move a couple of yards to the left. Or take cover."

It was nonsense. It was total nonsense, but Valier bought it. Or at least he considered the danger. Through the security cameras I saw the EMSOs in front of the main doors move, looking around them, and in their midst, I glimpsed Valier himself.

"Perhaps a discussion is warranted," said Valier.

"Come on inside and we'll have ourselves a little chat," said Tanner.

Valier chuckled. "I am not that gullible, Mr. Tanner. You may come outside, and we'll speak. I will permit you to say your piece and then return to the administrative building. If you wish, you can bring two or three of your companions for security." His voice hardened. "Just so long as two of them are Colonel Cassius Argent and Ian Royale."

"Why?" said Tanner.

"I would very much like to speak with them," said Valier. "There are certain matters that merit discussion."

Tanner looked at Argent and Mr. Royale, who both nodded.

"Fine," said Tanner. "We'll meet you outside in half an hour."

"Make it fifteen minutes," said Valier. "My guests will get impatient, and I might wish to entertain them with a fireworks display." Valier's chuckle echoed over the speakers. "I suggest you be on time."

The call cut off with a click and a burst of static.

"Right," muttered Tanner. "Charles, any idea how long it will take for the tromosaurs to show up?"

"I do not know, Security Director Tanner," said Charles. "The tromosaurs will almost certainly respond to the hunting call at once, but there is a considerable distance from the fence to Outpost Town proper. It may take them some time for them to follow the frequencies here."

"He's probably lying," I said. "If we step outside, he'll try to kill us."

"Maybe," said Tanner. "We can make it harder for him, though. There is a small armory in the security station here with some grenades, and we can take those. Plus, the longer we keep him talking, the longer we have." He looked at Mr. Royale and Argent. "If he wants to talk to you, I assume it's because he wants something from you. The longer we can keep him fishing for it, the better our odds."

"I'll go with you," I said.

Mr. Royale frowned. "You're volunteering? We might well get shot."

"Yeah," I said. I didn't want to mention that getting shot was a better way to die than getting eating by a tromosaur. "Well, I want to see this to the end. Plus, I did spray a mustache on Valier's face. Maybe I'll get to try the real thing."

Tanner snorted. "You're an optimist, Spraycan. Let's go."

We hastened through the corridors of the administrative building. Tanner unlocked the door to the security station, and we equipped ourselves with grenades. We also took pistols, since they were quicker to aim than the heavy Avengers, though we kept our rifles slung over our shoulders as well. The pistols only held fifteen rounds in their magazines, not nearly as many as the Avengers, but even with the Avengers, Valier had us outnumbered and outgunned.

After arming ourselves, we stopped in one of the offices behind the lobby.

"All right," said Tanner, handing a tablet to Charles. "This will give you lock/unlock control over the front doors. Let us out, and then lock the doors behind us again. Don't let us in again until it's clear. Keep an eye out on the video."

I swallowed as Charles took the tablet.

"I will follow your instructions to the letter, Security Director Tanner," said Charles.

Tanner grinned and the two men shook hands. "I know you will, Hiram."

"Mulger, Thompkins, cover us from inside," said Argent. Both Security Ministry officers still had their rifles out. "If this goes bad, be sure to take out Valier."

"Sir," said Mulger.

With exactly one minute left, we walked into the lobby. The massive doors of transparent metal stood closed, and through them I saw the glare of the Arborean afternoon. The glare served to illuminate the dozens of EcoMin operatives standing in the street outside the administrative building, along with about a dozen of the bodyguards of Valier's various guests. A few of them were overequipped posers like Toulon's bodyguards. But some of them were older, and looked like combat vets more dangerous than any EMSO.

Charles unlocked the doors, and I followed Tanner, Argent, and Mr. Royale into the street. A moment later the doors thumped locked behind us. We walked a few paces into the street and stopped, and every single gun the EMSOs and bodyguards had in hand was aimed at us.

I remembered a video I had seen as a kid, a story about a showdown in the street on ancient Earth and hoped no one was feeling trigger-happy.

Four of the EMSOs marched forward, flanking Ecology Minister Paul Valier as he stopped a dozen yards from us.

I had seen him from a distance several times, but up close, he looked almost exactly like his portrait, tall and lean and commanding. His elegant suit looked as if it had cost as much as Uncle Morgan's farm would have commanded on the open market, and his dark eyes were amused as he looked us over.

"Well, well," said Valier. "Colonel Cassius Argent. I should have known you would have been behind this. You've been nipping at my heels for years, like a dog chasing a truck. Of course, you know what happens to the dog that catches the truck." He clapped his hands together. "The Transport Ministry scrapes it off the road the next day."

"Big words," said Argent, "from a man who likes to shoot at people who can't shoot back."

"Don't be absurd, Colonel," said Valier. "That's the best time to shoot at people."

"You would know," said Argent.

"Well, yes, I would," said Valier. "That's the entire point."

"A corrupt criminal like you," said Argent.

"Criminal?" said Valier, his amusement plain. "Colonel, you miss the entire point of my efforts. Do you really think I'm doing this for personal enrichment?"

"Yes," said Argent, Tanner, and Mr. Royale in unison. I blinked and then nodded my agreement.

"How very small-minded of you," said Valier. "But I shouldn't be surprised. You are all small-minded men." He pointed at Argent. "The policeman, carrying out laws he is too stupid and stubborn to understand." The finger shifted to Tanner. "The hired thug, too stupid even to make it as a policeman." His finger moved to Mr. Royale. "And the capitalist." He frowned at me. "I don't know who you are, boy."

"I defaced your official portrait," I said.

Valier blinked, a little surprised, and promptly decided to ignore me. "You are all small-minded men of little vision."

"So why don't you tell us about that vision?" said Argent.

Valier kept talking. That surprised me, but maybe it shouldn't have. The man was a politician, so obviously he was fond of the sound of his own voice. And as a politician, he was a professional liar. I had the feeling he found it refreshing to tell the truth for once.

"I am saving humanity," he said, "and I am saving the interstellar environment from humanity. We are rather like an interplanetary virus. We have spread, and spread, and spread until there is no corner of the Thousand Worlds that we have not touched, no natural environment that we have left unaltered. Mankind is a disease, a plague, a pestilence to be managed, from the macroplanetary perspective."

"Right," said Tanner, his skepticism plain.

Valier kept talking, his eyes coming alive with passion, and his gestures became more and more animated. I realized that he really believed what he was saying.

"There are too many excess and useless people," he said. "Far, far too many. We need to reduce the human population drastically, if we are to restore the interstellar environment to its pristine state. That is the real reason for Safari Company, Argent, the reason you were too blind to see. The excess human population desperately needs to be managed and culled… and what better way to do it than to get rid of a few reactionaries in the process?"

"Like me, I assume?" said Mr. Royale.

Valier sneered at him. "You, and your detestable machines! They have defaced the streets of Wilson City. Everywhere I go, I see those vile machines crouching upon the street corners like ugly, garish, metal mushrooms! Everywhere! It is appalling. You wax fat upon the useless eaters, and line your pockets on the backs of a population fit only for culling!"

"Lining my pockets?" said Mr. Royale. "I'm not the one organizing murder hunts on unpopulated planets for millions of credits a pop."

"And you say there are too many humans anyway," said Tanner. "Royale's just feeding them. Someone's got to do it! Granted, maybe KwikBreets aren't my first choice for lunch…"

"Winston!" said Mr. Royale, sounding betrayed.

"But he's feeding people," said Tanner. "You just want to kill them."

"Feeding useless people useless, low-quality garbage," said Valier. "It's all an exercise in recycling waste!"

"Low quality?" said Mr. Royale. He seemed more offended by that than anything else Valier had said so far. "Low quality? I will have you know we spend *months* negotiating for the best prices on the highest-quality ingredients, and…"

"Shut up," said Valier.

Mr. Royale kept talking. "And I personally visited over seventeen farms in search of the best prices on wheat for the tortillas, and as for the teriyaki sauce, I–"

"Shut up, you filthy predator!" said Valier. "I don't care about your stupid grease cylinders. No. This is about the future. A future where mankind is properly controlled and governed and contained, and where men like you," he gave a disdainful gesture in our direction, "are obsolete and unnecessary."

"If that's true," said Tanner, "then why are you talking to us in the first place?"

"Because," said Valier, "I'm going to give you a choice."

"And what choice is that?" said Argent.

"Those three shuttles that took off earlier," said Tanner. "Tell them to land and surrender, now."

"Or what?" said Tanner.

I thought I saw something move behind the rows of EMSO soldiers, and I tensed. At the same time, there was a scream somewhere in the distance. Tanner and Argent exchanged a look, and Tanner nodded. They'd heard it too.

"Or," said Valier with a wide smile, "I'm going after your families. Almost all of the employees of Safari Company have family back on New Princeton, don't they? And all your men have families back home, don't they, Colonel Argent? All those women and children with lives and careers and dreams, all of them so easy to shatter. We won't execute them, there is no need for that. We'll just drive them to despair and self-destruction, perhaps even suicide. I'll have their assets seized, their property forfeited for environmental crimes, real or manufactured. I'll have them driven from their jobs, and if they're on Basic Income, I'll put so many restrictions on them that they'll wind up in prison. Look, you know you are all walking dead men already. Surrender now, and I'll leave them alone. Resist, and you'll all die anyway, and guarantee the destruction of the lives of every single person related to every last Safari Company employee."

I saw more flickers of movement behind the EcoMin operators and the bodyguards. All the hair on the back of my neck stood up.

"Hey," I said. "Tanner. I think you should call Charles. I think you should call Charles now. Right now."

Tanner frowned at me, and then his eyes widened.

"Yeah," he said, taking several steps back. "All right, I don't think we're going to do that, Valier. It's been nice talking to you. You're just as charming as everyone says."

Valier frowned. "Where do you think you're going?" He was clearly confused by Tanner's sudden change of demeanor.

"Back inside," said Tanner.

Valier shook his head. "You're not going anywhere." He gestured, and the four Ministry men flanking him lifted their weapons.

Right then, three different tromosaur packs attacked in unison.

I wasn't sure, but I think they had been creeping up the street during the negotiations. Valier's men hadn't been watching for them, of course, and the tromosaurs' stealthiness allowed them to move unseen through the town. Suddenly, the air on the street rippled, and the sleek black forms of dozens of tromosaurs appeared. They hit the EMSOs from behind, and in a heartbeat more than a dozen of them went down, tromosaur claws ripping at their armor to get at the flesh beneath. Shots rang out, followed by screams, but the shooting was haphazard and ineffective. Two or three tromosaurs went down, but the off-worlders didn't know what they were fighting, or how to fight them, and so the advantage of surprise was with the alien predators.

In that instant, the orderly scene in the street dissolved into bloody howling chaos as more tromosaurs rippled into sight, leaping into the fray. They were already in a feeding frenzy, and in that state they wouldn't stop hunting and killing for anything.

In that instant, Valier's expression transformed from smug contempt to naked shock. He was too astonished to even be afraid.

Yeah, being the hunted is way less fun than being the hunter, isn't it?

"Charles!" roared Tanner, and we turned and ran for the doors. We had planned to take prisoners, but it was obvious that had been a futile idea. The tromosaurs were ripping through the soldiers and the bodyguards and the various guests like a hailstorm through one of Uncle Morgan's wheat fields, and if we didn't get inside right away, we were going to die alongside them.

We sprinted towards the doors as screams and shouts and roars and gunfire crescendoed behind us. I heard the clang as the doors unlocked, saw Mulger and Thompkins hurrying to push them open. Their guns came up, and for a moment I thought they were aiming right at us, but then they opened fire, covering our retreat. I glanced back and saw Valier spin and cry out as a round struck him in the shoulder, but I also saw a tromosaur rushing towards me, its evil yellow eyes fixated on me. I didn't know it was possible for me to run any faster, but I managed it anyhow.

We reached the doors and threw ourselves through the gap as Mulger and Thompkins pulled them closed. Charles locked them with a loud clang, and an instant later I heard the thump as a tromosaur slammed into the transparent metal behind me, its claws squealing as it raked them across the doors. I felt it glare at me through the doors, but it didn't glare for long.

Not when there was fresh meat at hand. Valier had pushed himself back up and was staggering in our direction, one hand pressed against the gunshot wound in his shoulder, the other reaching out towards us in desperation.

The beast turned and leaped upon Valier. When it started to feed, even Argent looked away.

"I think," said Tanner at last, "we had better turn the fence back on."

I did. It didn't help much. Hundreds of tromosaurs were already inside the fence, and there were hundreds of prey for them to hunt within the perimeter of Outpost Town. The surviving EcoMin men retreated to one of the buildings across the street, a utility garage that housed landscaping drones. As a defensive position, it was terrible. Most of the garage doors were open, and the smaller doors had large glass windows. The tromosaurs methodically encircled it, battering at the windows, and sometimes I saw flashes of gunfire as the trapped men within opened fire. More than once, a panicked man burst out from the doors, trying to flee for his life. I have no idea where they thought they were going.

It was stupid. The tromosaurs had no trouble running them down.

"It appears the tromosaurs are breaking into two groups," said Charles, looking through the doors with a pair of collapsible binoculars he had produced from a pocket. "One group is attacking the utility garage, and I suspect the rest are trying to find their way into the convention hall."

Tanner grunted. "The largest number of prey in both those places, I suppose."

"I'm just glad we got most of our people into the air," said Mr. Royale.

"Yeah," said Tanner. "Those creatures will kill anything they find."

"How many tromosaurs are out there?" said Argent.

"Unknown," said Charles. "I have counted a minimum of five hundred so far. Given that they have no fear of humans, and they metabolize human flesh quite easily, I suspect we may have lured as many as a thousand of them into Outpost Town."

"A thousand?" said Mulger. His eyes were a little wild. "Can they get in here?"

"Quite possibly," said Charles. "We shall have to remain vigilant."

"Yeah," said Thompkins. "The system says all the doors leading in here are locked, but I'm going to go check them personally just in case."

He ran doors leading to the office wings and the server rooms as another dozen tromosaurs ran past the transparent main doors. Some of them disappeared from sight as they slipped into stealth mode, while others glared at us through the transparent metal, their eyes like sulfurous jewels.

"Colonel," said Tanner. "You'd better warn your men before they land."

"I warned them about the possibility. They know they're heading into a dangerous situation," said Argent. "And they have power armor."

"A warning is not sufficient preparation to hunt tromosaurs effectively," said Charles. "Especially in these numbers."

Argent scowled. "Then what do you suggest, Mr. Charles?"

"Hey, wait," I said. "Your ship's a gunship, right? What kind of guns does it have?"

Argent and Tanner shared a look.

"It's a standard Security Ministry gunship," said Argent. "Technically classified as a corvette. It's equipped with ship-to-ship missiles, plasma cannons, and rail guns."

"That kind of weaponry used in Outpost Town," said Tanner, "might wind up leveling Outpost Town. We'd kill all the tromosaurs, sure, but no one else would survive."

"What if the tromosaurs were all in one place?" I said.

"That would work," said Argent. "*Mathey* is atmosphere-capable. If the creatures are in a relatively confined space, the plasma cannons could wipe out a lot of them with minimal damage to the rest of Outpost Town."

"Minimal damage?" said Mr. Royale.

Argent shrugged. "We might burn down a building or two. But nothing too serious. The gunners on the ship know their job. We came here to arrest Valier, not to cause civilian casualties."

"Great," said Tanner. "But how are we going to get the tromosaurs into one place?"

"Their hunting cry," I said, digging out the thick tablet once more. "That's how we got them all into Outpost Town in the first place."

"We don't have a PA system loud enough to draw them to one place," said Tanner.

"The quadcopters," said Charles.

We all looked at him, and Charles shrugged.

"Both our quads and those belonging to EcoMin are equipped with external speaker systems," said Charles. "We could use them to broadcast the hunting call loud enough to lure the tromosaurs after the vehicle in relative safety."

"We get them all to gather," said Tanner, "and the gunship blasts them from above."

"Yes," said Charles.

"Great," said Argent. "But where is the nearest quad?"

"Let me see," said Tanner. He jogged over to the receptionist's desk, sat down with a grunt, and unlocked the computer. A moment later he had logged into the remote access for the security cameras, cycling through the blue-tinted images with practiced speed.

"There," he said, pointing at the screen. "Hangar Three, at the other end of the main administrative street. We still have a quadcopter there. Doesn't look damaged."

"Getting there will be hard," I said. "That's nearly a kilometer of open street from here to Hangar Three. If we try to take it on foot, the tromosaurs will run us down."

"A jeep," said Charles. "There still should be some in the garage here."

"Yeah," said Tanner, the display on the screen changing to the garage. "A couple of the electric jeeps are still there. We can take one to Hangar Three, get the quadcopter into the air, and lure the tromosaurs into the Security Ministry's guns."

"All right," said Argent. "I'll call Captain Butler and warn him not to land anyone, and to stand by for further orders once they're over the town. Mulger, you'll go with Tanner and Charles. You're the only one here who knows how to fly a quadcopter."

"I crashed the last two quadcopters I flew," protested Mulger.

"Third time's the charm," said Argent.

"I'll go with them, too," I said. The others all looked at me, and I tapped the thick tablet I had used to control the cleaning drones. "I've got all the tromosaurs' calls on here. I can plug this into the quadcopter's computer and take over its PA system." I shrugged. "That, and another gun can't hurt."

"No, it can't," said Tanner. "All right. Sam, Charles, and Mulger, you're with me. Argent, Ian, you're in charge here. Once we're in the air, we'll call you, and we'll coordinate with the gunship."

"Good luck, all of you," said Mr. Royale. He smiled a little. "I admit this wasn't what I had in mind when I hired you, Sam."

"Well," I said. "It's not like you actually pay me."

"I may have to reconsider that."

"Let's move," said Tanner.

We left the lobby, sealing the door behind us, and jogged through the hallways of the administrative building. Charles stopped at a security station to retrieve more weapons and supplies, and we hurried the rest of the way to the garage. A few of the four-seater electric jeeps were still in place, which was good, but the garage doors were open, which was bad. I had feared that some of the tromosaurs might have gotten into the garage, and two of them prowled across the oil-stained concrete, their heads snapping around to face us as we entered the garage.

In unison both tromosaurs charged at us, and in unison all four of us raised our weapons and fired. We took down the tromosaurs with a volley of concentrated fire, bullets ripping through their skulls and chests, and both animals fell to the floor, but not before they both let out ear-splitting shrieks.

"Think the others heard that?" said Tanner.

"Almost certainly," said Charles with perfect calm, reloading his Avenger. "That was the alarm cry. The nearest beasts will soon be converging on our location to assess the threat and neutralize it."

"Sonic alarms?" I said.

"The tromosaurs will not be able to hear them over the engine noise," said Charles.

Tanner said several bad words. "Run!"

We hurried to the nearest jeep and threw ourselves into the vehicle. Tanner dropped into the driver's seat, while Mulger and Charles took the back seat. I braced my gun on the side of the vehicle, hoping to use it to stabilize my aim.

"Right," said Tanner, starting the engine. Electric motors normally did not make a lot of noise, but the engine in the tough little jeep was powerful enough to give off a loud hum. I found hard to believe it could block our sonic alarms, but it was best to assume that it would. "Mulger, watch the right, Charles, you cover the left and back. Sam, shoot anything coming at us and try to keep our path clear."

"The top-rated speed of this vehicle is fifty miles an hour," said Charles. "Tromosaurs can exceed that in short bursts."

"Then you had better shoot them before they get to us," said Tanner. He slammed on the accelerator, and the jeep hurtled backward. He spun the wheel, the tires squealing against the concrete, and the jeep slewed around to point at the open garage doors.

The air outside the garage doors was rippling with the effect of the tromosaurs' stealth ability.

"Tanner!" I said.

"Hang on!" Tanner said, and he slammed on the accelerator.

The jeep howled forward. After you've traveled on interstellar starships and flown in hunting quadcopters, fifty miles an hour shouldn't seem that fast. But when you're in a garage driving at a group of hunting tromosaurs, fifty miles an hour feels completely out of control. I swung my

Avenger around and started shooting, and I think I must have hit one of the tromosaurs, because it dropped its stealth and came at us, screeching, and Charles shot it through the head.

We slammed into the charging tromosaurs, and the jeep bucked as if the engine had exploded. One of the tromosaurs became visible, screeching in outrage, and it hit the hood, bounced off the windshield, flipped over our heads, and landed behind the jeep. I don't think the impact killed it because at once it started to climb to its feet. Fortunately, the jeep had been built to survive the harsh environment of Arborea, and while the tromosaur had dented the fender, it hadn't damaged the engine. I managed to shoot another tromosaur as we sped past, then Tanner spun the wheel again, the tires screamed, and the jeep rocketed down the street behind the administrative building, heading for Hangar Three.

"Where did you learn to drive?" I said, twisting around to look back at the administrative building. We had broken free of the tromosaur pack, but a dozen of the predators were in front of the garage, all of them running after us. They weren't running at their full speed, which meant that they hadn't yet decided if they were going to chase us or not. If they did, they might run us down in short order. We were putting distance between us, but not as much as I would like.

"Wilson City!" shouted Tanner over the roar of the wind. "I failed the test three times."

"What?" I said.

Mulger and Charles had rotated around in their seats to watch the tromosaurs.

"Maybe it was four times," said Tanner.

I started to protest again, and then the tromosaurs vanished into ripples as their hides began the biochemical stealth reaction that they used to vanish.

"Aw, man," I said, and I raised my Avenger, sighting along the side of the jeep so I wouldn't hit Charles or Mulger, and I started shooting. Because of the of stealth ability, I wasn't sure if I was actually hitting anything or not.

Nonetheless, the blurs were getting closer.

Charles raised a black tube, and I recognized the rocket launcher he had used earlier.

"You were able to reload that thing?" I said.

"Yes," announced Charles, and he squeezed the trigger. The launcher vomited out a plume of white smoke, soon left behind with our speed, and the rocket slammed into the blurs, erupting in a ball of fire. Five tromosaurs snapped back into view, two of them on fire, and three of them hurtling through the air from the blast of the explosion. The rest of the tromosaurs slowed, and Mulger and I kept shooting, hoping to keep the tromosaurs at bay.

It worked. The tromosaurs slowed long enough for Tanner's reckless driving to cover the rest of the distance, and soon I saw the sturdy gray mass of Hangar Three come into sight. I also spotted several other tromosaurs wandering around outside, and Charles, Mulger, and I started shooting. We managed to account for five between the three of us, but the rest of them began to home in on us.

Tanner drove into the hangar at full speed, slammed on the brakes, and spun the wheel around. We skidded to a halt next to one of the remaining quadcopters, the tromosaurs racing into the hangar after us.

"Sonic alarms!" barked Charles, and we activated our sonic alarms. The incoming tromosaurs slowed as their instincts assessed the new threat, but they did not slow for long. Tanner hammered at the door control, entering a code, and the quadcopter's passenger door swung open.

We scrambled inside just as the tromosaurs overcame their indecision and attacked. Charles and I covered the door, sending out bursts of fire, while Tanner slapped at the door control and Mulger scrambled into the pilot's cabin.

"Think they can get in here?" I said.

"Given enough time, they can get inside almost any structure," said Charles.

As if to confirm his words, I heard a clang, and a large dent appeared in the door.

"Get up here and strap in!" said Mulger. "This is going to be the shortest and sloppiest preflight check in the history of aviation, but we are taking off."

We scrambled into the pilot cabin. I dropped into the copilot's seat and started helping Mulger with the preflight check as fast as I could. I wanted to simply take off, but this model of quadcopter refused to fly until at least the minimum preflight check had been completed. I had excellent motivation to hurry because I saw a dozen tromosaurs through the windows in the pilot cabin. The windows were made of transparent metal alloy, but I wouldn't put it past the tromosaurs to punch through them, or to simply knock the panes out of the frames.

"Fuel pumps three and four?" said Mulger.

"Ready," I said, watching the indicators go from red to green.

At that moment one of the tromosaurs jumped forward and slammed into the canopy two feet from my face. I felt the shudder through the deck from the animal's impact and heard the squeal of its claws as they ground into the transparent metal. The canopy held, but the tromosaur had left a row of bright scratches in the metal. One tromosaur would not have been able to break inside, but if they decided to attack in a systematic way, we were done.

"Better hurry," said Tanner.

"Hurrying," barked Mulger, and he slapped a row of switches.

The quadcopter shuddered as the engines and the fuel pumps came to life. A message flashed across the main display, informing us that the manufacturer did not approve of the expedited preflight checklist and that we had just voided the warranty by doing so. Mulger gripped the throttles, and the quadcopter jerked forward as the rotors spun up, lifting the craft a few yards into the air. The tromosaurs backed away, alarmed by the sudden sound, and Mulger sent the quadcopter gliding forward.

The tromosaurs were mostly out of the way, but one, more curious or stupid than the others, got in the way. We hit it dead center of the canopy, where it clung there for a moment, suspended like an oversized insect with its arms and legs outstretched. Mulger cursed and revved the engine, and we flew out of the hangar, missing the top of the door by a few feet, and into the open air over Outpost Town. The tromosaur on the canopy held on for a few seconds longer, lost its grip, and fell to the ground below.

I looked down. Even the fall didn't kill the monster. It merely regained its footing, shook itself, and went off in search of easier prey.

"Sam, call Argent," said Tanner.

"Right," I said. I tapped my earpiece, linked it to the quadcopter's transmitters and computer, and called for Argent. "Colonel?"

"Here," came Argent's voice. "Status?"

"We're in the air," I said. I tapped a few commands on the control board to send Argent's voice through the quadcopter's speakers. "We had to outrun a few tromosaurs to do it, but we've got a quadcopter."

"Good," said Argent. "I'm coordinating with the ship. They're coming in over the water from the west. You should be able to see them now at about ninety degrees, I think."

I twisted around to look in the direction of the ocean, and I did indeed see the distant shape of the Security Ministry gunship. It looked a bit like a stylized black dagger, dark from stealth armor, and it seemed to get bigger even as I looked. It was coming in fast.

"You have visuals on any of the tromosaurs?" said Tanner.

"Looks like there's a big group still outside the administrative building," said Mr. Royale. "Probably another group around the convention hall."

"I've got an idea," I said. "Why don't we fly over the convention hall first and play their hunting cry? Then we can lure the tromosaurs there after us, fly to the administrative building, and then lead the whole bunch of them out into the empty fields. Then the gunship can vaporize them without blowing up Outpost Town."

There was silence for a moment.

"Sounds good to me, Hammond," said Argent. "All right. Mulger, broadcast your ID, let the gunship know where you are."

"Yes, sir," said Mulger, flipping switches on the communications panel. "Heading for the convention hall. Hammond, you'd better get that call ready."

"Right," I said, digging the chunky tablet from my belt. The quadcopter banked over Outpost Town, heading for the convention hall, and I linked the tablet to the quadcopter's computer. A moment later I brought up the tromosaurs' hunting call, feeding it into the quadcopter's PA system. "Ready."

"Here we go," said Mulger, turning the quadcopter over the convention hall. The convention hall had twelve sets of fancy transparent-metal doors, and in front of those doors were hundreds of tromosaurs, all of them hammering to get inside. The sight of one tromosaur was frightening. The sight of such a massive pack of them was terrifying.

Man, I was glad I was high above them in the quadcopter!

"All right, Sam," said Tanner. "Let's invite them on a hunt, shall we?"

"Right," I said and tapped the command on the tablet.

Even inside the quadcopter, even through the roar of the rotors, I heard the hunting cry bellow from the craft's speakers.

"Loud," muttered Mulger. "But is it loud enough?"

As one, every single tromosaur outside the convention hall lifted its head to look at us.

Now that was a sight to test the spine of the bravest man.

"Mulger," said Tanner. "Let's take them for a walk."

Mulger swooped the quadcopter low, just low enough to stay out of reach of the tromosaurs' leaps, and flew over the street towards the administrative building. The tromosaurs ran after us, hundreds of them, and more of the creatures boiled from the alleys between the buildings. We flew over the mob of tromosaurs outside the administrative building, and they looked skyward, joining the mass of predators as they surged after us.

Then we were outside of Outpost Town, flying over the cleared fields towards the jungle.

"How many?" said Tanner.

"At least five hundred," said Charles. "Possibly more."

I turned my head and saw the gunship flying overhead, a black shadow against the alien sky of Arborea.

"Sir," said Mulger. "I think we're ready. Does the gunship have targets?"

"Yes," said Argent. "You're at a safe distance, Mulger. Gunners, you are clear to fire."

The Security Ministry gunship started firing plasma shells at the tromosaurs.

They were on the lowest power setting, Argent explained, so weak they would have been useless for ship-to-ship combat.

Nonetheless, from the vantage point of the quadcopter, it looked as if God had decided to start raining fire down upon Arborea.

There was a brilliant flare of white light, and then a roar as a line of fire erupted from the field and engulfed the tromosaurs. Mulger snarled and yanked the quadcopter's stick as the shock wave buffeted the craft, and sent us banking back towards Outpost Town. Through the canopy, I saw a massive lake of roaring fire, and no trace of the tromosaurs.

"Cease fire," said Argent. "Mulger, status?"

"I think that did the trick, sir." He sounded more than a little awed. I know I was.

"It is possible we are the first humans to successfully hunt tromosaurs using plasma-based weaponry," said Charles.

"I wouldn't recommend it for trophy-hunting," Mr. Royale observed.

"Yeah, we made history," said Argent his voice hardening. "Come on in and land at the administrative building. Royale tells me there's an empty helipad on the roof. I'll tell the gunship to land by the convention hall, and we'll want your help to deal with any surviving tromosaurs. You want to make history, Mr. Charles? Well, we're about to arrest half the richest men and women from twenty different worlds. We're going to make a whole lot of history before we're done."

We landed on the helipad and assisted the power-armored Security Ministry officers as they disembarked. As it turned out, the plasma barrage had wiped out most of the tromosaurs, so there wasn't much left for us to do.

So I was there when SecMin Colonel Cassius Argent arrested a whole lot of very rich, very terrified people.

Chapter 10

Colony Company

Arborea was all but destroyed. And as a result, New Princeton was in political disarray.

We didn't start a revolution, and we didn't exactly cause the overthrow of the Acadarchy, but I think we indirectly triggered something of a coup. Without Valier at the helm, the other Ministries went after the Ecology Ministry with all the ravenous glee of a starving tromosaur, and the Security Ministry carried out mass arrests of EcoMin's leadership. It turned out that a few officials had known about Valier's little human hunts, and considerably more ministry employees had their hands in the till in one way or another.

I think we also sparked an amount of economic upheaval across the Thousand Worlds. Many of Valier's guests had been extremely wealthy and extremely powerful men, right up until they found out that tromosaurs respected neither wealth nor power. The deaths of executives from twenty-six of the Thousand Worlds' most powerful companies caused a lot of infighting, the implosion of some companies, arrests at others, and many official disavowals of their recently devoured CEOs and chairmen.

So, while there wasn't a revolution or a military coup or anything like that, before the disaster at Arborea one set of people were in charge of the Acadarchy, and after the disaster a new set of people were in charge. Most of the former were either in prison, were discovered to have committed suicide with a bullet to the back of the head, or had voluntarily resigned in haste to spend more time with their families. That was probably how I found myself with my new job.

But I'm getting ahead of myself. Let's get back to Arborea for a bit.

Argent's men were good at their job. Once we had cleared Outpost Town of the last of the tromosaurs, the SecMin agents started searching for survivors. It turned out there were more than we'd expected. Only a few of the guests had accompanied Valier to watch him deal with us and shared his fate. Many other, however, had thought it was more fun to stay in the air-conditioned convention hall and watch the proceedings via video, so they got to watch in comfort as Valier and his men got eaten. Argent's men found them there and arrested the lot of them.

Most of them were billionaires, with a few trillionaires in the mix, so they all had the very best lawyers money could buy. Unfortunately for them, there was one obstacle no amount of legal chicanery could overcome.

Valier had left behind an absolute mountain of evidence.

His apparent sloppiness made sense when you considered that he planned to kill every last employee of Safari Company and destroy all of the evidence with Outpost Town. But Valier got himself killed before he could get around to that, and Tanner's security cameras recorded everything. Also, Argent's men took over Valier's shuttle and found that the former Ecology Minister had kept meticulous records. Even without the video evidence, the records were enough to seal the fate of Valier's guests and seven EcoMin vice-ministers. Theresa's mother wasn't one of them, though, and I was kind of glad about that.

But something very interesting was revealed in Valier's records.

It was the *second time* he had done this.

It turned out it wasn't even his idea originally. He was carrying on a program that had been designed by the previous Ecology Minister as a method of population control. Valier's insight was that the vulnerable state of any human colony on Arborea would allow him to repeat the lethal game there as many times as he could wipe the slate clean.

Mr. Royale quoted some old Earth book about how the schemer falls into the pit which he digs for another—Mr. Royale does like his old Earth books—but Kayla only said in a quiet voice that it was just as well she hadn't gotten her hands on Valier.

For those of us who survived the destruction of Safari Company, we didn't get in too much trouble, which kind of surprised me. I had to give a lot of interviews to various Security Ministry investigators, and I was questioned very closely about the sonic fence, but the investigators concluded that everything we had done had been justifiable self-defense. It probably helped that half the leadership of the Security Ministry had been after Valier for a long time. Colonel Argent even got promoted to vice-minister for interplanetary relations.

At first, I went back to repairing KwikBreet machines and delivery vans for Mr. Royale's company. Hoskins took over as his general manager, and Hiram Charles got a job with the Security Ministry in charge of overseeing dangerous wildlife. Tanner and Kayla returned to New Princeton as well, with Tanner moving into private security work, and Kayla writing technical manuals about quadcopters. One of the dead Safari employees had left behind an orphaned baby girl, and after much legal rigmarole, Tanner and Kayla adopted her. Kayla seemed pretty happy, and even Tanner seemed less surly than usual. I was pretty sure parenthood suited them, and that they would wind up adopting a second one sooner rather than later.

I was glad to be alive, but it wasn't long before I was getting kind of bored. As awful as it is surviving quad-crashes and slogging through the jungle, getting bitten by blood-sucking bugs and being attacked by vicious predators both human and inhuman, it turns out that it's hard to go back to an ordinary life after that. Nothing really seemed to matter all that much anymore.

I still didn't like Wilson City very much. At one point Theresa even got in touch with me, wondering if we could get together, but I deleted the message and blocked her. I wasn't that bored, and besides, it would be safer to date a tromosaur.

But then Mr. Royale asked me to join his new business venture.

One of the things that changed along with the leadership of the Acadarchy was their attitude towards establishing new colonies. New Princeton had not founded a colony in decades, thanks to the Ecology Ministry's negative opinion on the matter, but Valier's downfall had changed things. Now the Acadarchy was chartering new colonies, offering them to the highest bidder… and with a little help from the new SecMin vice-minister Argent, he got a sweetheart deal. The Acadarchy had rights to a planet a few hundred light years away that featured an arid, but temperate climate, and they wanted to set up a colony there.

After calling in a few more favors, Mr. Royale had won the bid to establish that colony.

So that was how I became one of the founding members of the Tennent Colony Company. I wasn't the only Safari survivor either. Charles signed on as well, as did the Tanners and some of the others who had survived Arborea.

And to my very great surprise, Uncle Morgan sold the farm and signed on as well.

"It's a new world, Sam," said Uncle Morgan, clapping me on the shoulder. "Never thought I'd see the day. You and me, I think people like us were born to be out on the frontier. We don't belong here on a planet that's been tamed and domesticated for centuries. Maybe we'll make a mess of it, or maybe we'll build something great. Either way, I'm looking forward to finding out."

"I am, too," I said.

Even more surprising was when Mr. Royale appointed me Assistant Advance Team Leader. He came to see us off on our trip to complete the initial planetary survey and select a site on which to establish the first settlement. He said goodbye to the others, and saved me for last.

"I'd ask if you were ready for this, Sam, but I know you're more than equal to the challenge." He held out his hand and we shook. He had a firm grip.

"I appreciate your confidence in me, Mr. Royale. And I appreciate the way you're paying me this time even more."

He grinned. "Shoot straight and deal squarely, Sam, and not even the sky is the limit for you."

I didn't know what to say, so I just nodded and watched him walk away.

"Get a move on, Spraycan!" I heard someone call from behind me. "We've got a whole world waiting for us!"

It was Tanner. I laughed, picked up my bag, and turned to walk up the boarding ramp of the colony ship.

9 789527 065624